DOCTOR WHO
SURVIVAL

based on the BBC television series by Rona Munro
by arrangement with BBC Books, a division of BBC
Enterprises Ltd

RONA MUNRO

Number 150 in the
Target Doctor Who Library

A TARGET BOOK
published by
the Paperback Division of
W H Allen & Co Plc

A Target Book
Published in 1990
By the Paperback Division of
W H Allen & Co plc
338 Ladbroke Grove, London W10 5AH

The BBC producer of *Survival* was John Nathan-Turner
The director was Alan Wareing
The role of the Doctor was played by Sylvester McCoy

Printed and bound in Great Britain by
Cox & Wyman Ltd, Reading, Berks.

ISBN 0 426 20352 6

Chapter 1

It was an ordinary Sunday in Perivale. The hazy June sunshine made a half-hearted attempt to pierce the cloud and fumes that hung over London.

Mr Aitken was outside his home washing his car; he washed his car every Sunday. Inside the house, Mrs Aitken toiled over a turkey roast and a pan of mashed potato; they had a turkey roast every Sunday. Only the frozen vegetables varied: Mrs Aitken cooked either green beans or peas; occasionally she presented sweet-corn.

Mr Aitken was thinking about turkey roast and sweet-corn as he massaged suds into the bonnet of his car. The pink sponge moved in a hypnotic, regular rhythm. Mr Aitken was unaware that he was being observed.

On the opposite side of the street, a cat stared down at him from a window ledge. It was a powerful animal with heavy dark fur; it crouched with its head low, the tip of its tail twitching.

The cat regarded Mr Aitken as if he were a particularly plump and incautious sparrow. It watched as Mrs Aitken appeared in the neat front garden, flapping a tea-towel and calling her husband in for lunch. It waited until she had disappeared back into the house and the street was deserted except for Mr Aitken and his bucket of suds.

At first Mr Aitken didn't recognize the sound of hoofbeats. He was aware of a thundering clatter on the road behind him and a strange threatening animal noise – a throaty yowling. With the dripping sponge still his his hands, he turned to face the source of the noise, a frown on his face.

What he saw bearing down on him simply made no sense: his eyes saw it but his brain could not deal with the information. He gaped in shock until a delayed survival instinct propelled him up the street, breathless and stumbling.

Mrs Aitken heard his faint scream in the distance as she arranged paper napkins on the table in the front room. She moved to the window, opening it and leant out to call into the street, 'Dave?'

Mrs Aitken frowned. The car dripped, untended; an upturned bucket rolled in the gutter.

The cat slipped off the window ledge opposite and padded purposefully across the road to vanish behind a hedge.

Mrs Aitken pulled in her head and made for the door. She didn't see the cat, or the old-fashioned blue police box that then materialized at one side of her neat front garden. Even if she had she would have been unlikely to have identified it as a TARDIS, the time machine of a Time Lord, specifically the one belonging to the Doctor.

By the time Mrs Aitken reached the street the Doctor and his companion, Ace, had emerged. Ace was walking away down the road with the rapid, long strides of a woman who had had enough.

2

'You had to pick a Sunday didn't you?' Ace threw the words over her shoulder, 'You bring me back to boredom capital of the universe and you pick the one day of the week you can't even get a decent television programme.'

The Doctor followed a pace behind her, looking round at the sights. He was not familiar with Perivale in the late 1980s. He wasn't reacting to Ace's mood.

'As I recall Ace,' he murmured, 'I brought you here at your request.'

Ace swung round. 'I just said I wondered what the old gang were up to. You didn't need to bring us here did you? You could've dropped me up town and I could've phoned.'

They were now passing the Aitken's house. The Doctor glanced at the half-washed car. Mrs Aitken had walked down to the edge of the pavement and was looking anxiously up and down the road. The Doctor looked at her, taking in her expression. He bent down, picked up the overturned bucket and set it upright. Mrs Aitken barely noticed.

Ace sighed impatiently.

'I just wanted to catch up with a few mates, that's all, we didn't have to have the guided tour . . .' She strode off again. 'Come on, Professor.'

The Doctor followed meekly.

'So what's so terrible about Perivale?' he asked as he caught up with her.

Ace sighed again. 'Nothing ever happens here.'

Mrs Bates, the elderly woman at number thirty-three, a few doors down from the Aitkens, wasn't certain what was happening at the bottom of her garden: it sounded as if someone was killing a cat. She stared in

3

alarm at her herbaceous border which was thrashing to and fro as unseen animals struggled within it.

She pushed up her window and called 'Shoo!' plaintively and ineffectively as the yowls became screams. Abruptly there was silence. The bushes were motionless. A single cat slipped out of the undergrowth.

The woman gasped.

The cat looked up. Its eyes were red, as was its muzzle – red and dripping.

It was difficult to see anything attractive about the patch of wasteground to which Ace had led the Doctor. Dusty weeds struggled up through piles of split, black bin-liners that were stuffed with ancient rubbish. Ace stared at it all morosely. If this was home it still needed redecoration, she thought. It looked exactly as she remembered it. It was a depressing recollection. She looked at the Doctor.

'How long since I was here then?' she asked.

The Doctor considered a few complex descriptions of time and relativity. One of many inconveniences of time travel was the mind-boggling complexity of accurately describing any journey. He looked at the young woman he had taken half-way around the universe and into the past and future of this and several other planets. He decided to keep his explanation simple. 'You've been away exactly as long as you think you have.'

Ace snorted. 'Feels like I've been away for ever.'

She returned to her gloomy contemplation of the debris around her. The Doctor followed her gaze expectantly. It still appeared to be a singularly uninteresting and uninviting corner of twentieth century Earth. He sighed.

'Any particular reason for standing here?' he asked.

'It's Sunday.'

The Doctor attempted to make sense of this information and failed. He looked at her enquiringly.

'Some of the gang always come down here on Sunday.'

The Doctor looked round again. 'What for?'

The question seemed to irritate Ace; everything seemed to be irritating her. She kicked at the ground.

'I dunno . . . light a fire, muck about, you know.'

The Doctor stifled a yawn. She glared at him.

'Well I told you it was dull! Look, you don't need to hang about; I'll meet you back at the TARDIS if you want.'

The Doctor picked a dead head of willow herb and examined it briefly. If he had noticed her mood he wasn't reacting.

Ace sighed again.

'Maybe they don't come here anymore.' She spoke almost to herself, staring at a split bag with rotting and rotten rubbish. This was where she had come for fun and excitement – good times.

A threadbare tabby cat clawed at the plastic bag, widening its wounds.

'There's no one here is there?' she murmured. 'Nothing but tin cans and stray cats.'

'And horses.'

Ace looked at the Doctor in surprise. He was staring at the ground, still ignoring her. This was too irritating to be borne.

'Horses?' she snapped. 'In Perivale? Don't be stupid.'

Ace turned on her heel and strode off.

For a second the Doctor lingered, frowning at the hoofprint in the wet earth, then he followed her.

* * *

Perivale streets, a jungle of gutters, drainpipes, walls to leap, and brick that gave a good grip to paw-pads and claws. The cat slinked over garden gates, under the dark, oil-dripping shadows of parked cars. It stared, stalked and watched.

The cat saw red. Red eyes peered through a veil of blood at the shapes of these new creatures with their sharp, animal smell – food.

It stared out now at a flurry of legs that kicked round its hiding place. The cat listened to the shouts and blinked only at the thump of a football against the car that sheltered it. Its eyes were open wide, seeing all it could, showing what it saw.

On the other side of the door, the message was received. The strange cat had two pairs of eyes: one pair burned red in its own head; another pair was on the other side of the door. They were cat's eyes in the head of a creature that was nothing like the cat except for its hunger. Its eyes saw everything the cat saw; its eyes burned with the intelligence that spoke to it now.

'No, there is no sport for you here.'

The message whispered into the cat's dark brain from the other side of the door and it understood – too many to hunt, too much meat to kill. It slipped out from under the car and padded away.

The Doctor and Ace were just another pair of legs at the side of the football game. Their clumsy animal limbs meant nothing to the strange cat or to the other eyes that saw them at the edge of the strange cat's vision.

But the Doctor saw the cat. He turned from watching the group of boys energetically pursuing a football around him and frowned after the animal as it slid away up the street. He was still preoccupied when Ace re-emerged from the phone box behind him.

'There's no one home.'

She stared at him waiting for some response, agitatedly jingling the change she held.

This was not what Ace had imagined. She had expected to make a triumphant return – discreetly managed of course. Ace had dreamed of shocking old friends with a telephone call out of the blue and had imagined their shrieks of 'Ace, where have you been!?' She had practised her enigmatic grin, a reply that hinted at all of her extraordinary adventures but revealed nothing. She had come a long way since she left Perivale and she wanted to savour that change, but there was no one here who even knew she had ever lived in Perivale or that she had ever been away. Even her dark memories of the place seemed stale and distant.

It didn't make sense. Where was everyone? And couldn't the Doctor see she was upset?

With a sniff and a defensive twitch of her shoulders, Ace set off up the street again. She glanced over her shoulders at the Doctor.

'OK, last try. We'll go up the youth club.'

The Doctor nodded abstractedly and followed her.

There should have been a crowd spilling out the door of the youth club. Ace remembered the scene the last Sunday she had been there. Midge and Stevie had been engaged in a life and death struggle for the club's only pool cue. Two ghetto blasters had been going full blast as the music of Guns and Roses and that of Spondy Gee competed for attention. And Ace had been evading a crowd of girls led by Shreela who were intent on covering her in hair-spray. 'It'll be brilliant

7

Ace, we can put it all up on end, three feet high!' she remembered them saying.

Ace wasn't going to cramp her style by claiming maturity but that kind of carry on was something she had grown out of even then . . .

She stared at the youth club now. The door was still cracked where Midge had opened it with Ace's head; it swayed on its hinges, the only thing that moved. It looked even shabbier without a press of bodies to mask the ancient paintwork. It was deserted. She missed the noise; she missed the whole crowd of them.

'Where is everyone?'

The Doctor still didn't seem to be listening to her, although he looked as if he was listening to something. Ace impatiently pushed past him.

A series of doors opened off the lobby of the youth club. Ace began to fling them open one after another. She revealed a series of half-empty rooms, battered plastic chairs with one or two legs missing, and pale rectangles on the wall where posters used to hang.

'I mean it always was a dump but at least you could meet people. Look at this,' she pointed into a room where holes in the plaster showed some structure had been ripped off the wall. 'We used to have a coffee bar in here. What's happened to the coffee bar? Where is everyone?'

'Ace.'

She turned to look at him.

Finger to his lips, the Doctor pointed to the door she had yet to open.

Ace listened. She heard it too – the thudding of feet on the floor; grunts and pants of exertion. Ace took a step closer to the door. A dozen male voices suddenly yelled in unison.

Ace opened the door.

8

The room was windowless. Harsh strip lighting bleached and made bleak the faces of the young men inside the room. All of them were wearing T-shirts and track-suit bottoms. Sweat stained their clothes under their armpits and down the centre of their backs. The group was watching two young men who struggled in the centre of the floor. An older man bent over the fighters, his face red with excitement and exertion.

'Go on!'

The older man bellowed encouragement at point blank range. One of the fighters had the other pinned to the floor where he squirmed uselessly. The victor looked up.

'Go on, Stuart! What're you waiting for?' The older man stirred the winning fighter with his foot.

The boy shook his head. 'I've beat him Sergeant Paterson.'

The older man bent lower to speak straight into the boy's face. His voice was suddenly quiet and silky.

'What? You think we're playing games, do you? Let's pretend, eh? That what you're going to do to some villain, some mugger? Help him up, dust him down, shake hands?' he paused for effect then bellowed again. 'Go ON!'

It was a command. The young man obeyed. He cracked his companion's face against the floor and leapt away.

Ace winced and glanced at the Doctor. His face was impassive but she saw the lines of his mouth tighten.

The defeated boy lay groaning on the floor. Sergeant Paterson bent over him, patting at him as if the boy were a fallen animal.

'All right, lad, you're OK. On your feet now.'

He pulled the boy up. The youngster clutched his

face; blood trickled between his fingers. The sergeant patted him roughly.

'Come on, you're all right, eh?'

The boy spoke through his hands. 'Yes, sarge.'

Sergeant Paterson ruffled the boy's hair with heavy-handed affection.

'That's my boy. You go get cleaned up, eh?'

The boy stumbled out past Ace and the Doctor. Turning to watch him leave, the man saw the two strangers for the first time. He looked surprised for a second.

'I'll be right with you,' he said.

He turned back to the other young men. They were still watching him silently and respectfully; only the boy who had won the fight stood separated a little from the rest. He was frowning at the floor.

'OK, shake hands lads. We'll see you on Friday.'

The boys turned to each other and shook hands. Only the one still stood apart from them. He glared at the sergeant.

'I'd already beat him, sarge.'

The older man stared back for a second then began to move in on him.

'Oh, I see. Think I'm too hard do you? Pushing you too hard am I? Ever heard of survival of the fittest son, eh? Ever heard of that? Life's not a game son, is it?'

Paterson was right on top of Stuart, staring into his face again, punctuating each question with a jab to the boy's stomach. The jabs got harder.

'I'm teaching you to survive, lad. I'm teaching you to fight back. What are you going to do when life starts pushing you around, eh? What are you going to do?'

The final jab swung at Stuart with all the weight of

the heavier man's body behind it. Stuart doubled over then swung back. He was furious.

Paterson blocked the wild, angry punches and laughed.

'That's my boy!'

Paterson ruffled Stuart's hair affectionately. As the boy still glowered at him, Paterson gripped his head and peered into Stuart's face.

'All right now, eh? All right?'

Stuart reluctantly grinned.

'All right, sarge.'

The other boys broke into whoops and cheers as if Stuart's surrender was the cue they'd been waiting for. They jogged out of the room, chorusing goodbyes to Paterson and directing punches at each other as they shouldered past the Doctor and Ace. Stuart jogged at their heels, smiling and shaking his head. The Doctor watched them go.

'Survival of the fittest,' murmured the Doctor, 'a rather glib generalization that is bound to be misinterpreted. I said as much to Charles at the time.'

He turned to Paterson. 'Fit for what, Sergeant Paterson?'

'Well, you show me a better way of surviving and I'll give it a go.' The Sergeant draped a towel around his neck and picked up a sports bag. 'Something I can help you with?'

Ace had already decided she recognized this plump, aggressive little man. Give him a uniform and she would be certain. She looked away and flicked her hair over half her face.

'I'm looking for some people,' she mumbled.

'What's that?' Paterson peered at her more closely. 'Don't I know you? I do, don't I?'

11

Ace sighed. Abandoning any attempt at disguise she tossed her hair back and stared at him defiantly.

Paterson nodded.

'That's right, let you off with a warning didn't we? You were lucky.'

'Erm . . . Ace, I think we have to be moving on now.' The Doctor made a move into the lobby.

Ace ignored him; she squared her shoulders and stared at Paterson.

'So where are the rest of them?'

'Who's that then?'

'Everyone! Everyone used to hang around in here on Sundays.'

'It's self-defence every Sunday afternoon now. That sorted the sheep from the goats, eh? I don't know where the wasters go now.'

Paterson turned away. He zipped up his sports bag, effectively dismissing her.

Ace turned to the Doctor for help.

'Professor, you ask him!'

But the Doctor wasn't listening. He was looking at a cat. And with its wide, red eyes the cat sat on the other side of the cracked, glass door and looked back at the Doctor.

The eyes that watched through the cat's widened in excitement as the intelligence behind them recognized a very different kind of prey. The hunter saw that his trap was baited and sprung; his quarry was already taking the first steps towards it.

Chapter 2

Still staring at the cat, the Doctor became dimly aware of the conversation between Ace and Paterson that continued behind him.

'No, I think you'll find most of your crowd have moved on.' Paterson sounded as if he had been glad to see the back of them.

'Moved on where?' Ace could barely keep her temper in check.

'Well, I think you'd have a better idea of that than me love, eh? Where have you been hiding yourself?'

'Around,' Ace said sullenly.

'Your mum had you listed as a missing person.'

The Doctor dragged his attention away from the strange cat and looked at the others. Ace's face was scarlet.

'Don't give a toss, do you?' Paterson looked her up and down, shaking his head. 'Four kids gone missing just this month – vanished into thin air.' He snorted. 'I don't know, it's the parents I feel sorry for. It doesn't take much to phone, love – ten pence that's all.'

Ace didn't even look at him. She made straight for

the glass door and slammed into it, rattling the cracked glass as she banged it open. The cat streaked for cover.

'Come on, Professor.'

She didn't look back to see if he was following; she stamped down the path from the youth club.

Paterson sighed and shook his head.

'I don't know, I wouldn't be that age again if you paid me, would you?'

The Doctor considered for a second. 'It's hard to remember; it was a long time ago.'

Politely he held the door open for Paterson as they left the club.

At the end of the path Ace shot the Doctor an angry glance. She waited with her back turned, one foot tapping angrily.

'What a world to be seventeen in, eh? I reckon you teach them to fight, that's all you can do. Then they'll fight or go under. Half of them go under anyway round here. They're past saving – wasters.' Paterson looked at the Doctor for agreement.

'Tell me, sergeant, do you have a problem with strays?

The Doctor's question seemed to bemuse the policeman.

'Strays?'

'Cats.'

Bemusement became disbelief. Paterson's tone was sarcastically formal.

'I wouldn't know, sir. It's hardly a police priority round here.'

'Hmm.' The Doctor looked around and pondered what he had seen.

At the end of the path Ace had had enough. She gave another glance to see if the Doctor was coming

14

then set off again, calling over her shoulder, 'Come on, Doctor!'

Paterson chuckled. 'Doctor, eh? You're not in the best of shape yourself though, are you?'

The Doctor looked at Paterson in surprise. 'What?'

'Well, my word for it would be scrawny, sir,' Paterson's chuckle deepended. 'You want to build yourself up Doc. I do a session down here Monday nights for the older men.'

Across the centuries, every Time Lord of necessity acquires a wide range of crushing retorts, insults and put-downs in the billions of languages of the universe. The Doctor looked at Paterson for a second, considered a few of them, but decided not to waste the effort.

'I must just go and see a man about a cat,' he murmured. He put on a burst of speed to catch up with Ace.

Paterson's voice pursued them.

'Keep fit and self-defence!'

'I don't believe it,' muttered Ace.

'One finger can be a deadly weapon!' Paterson's voice was receding now.

'And you know where you can put it.' Ace shot him a last, scornful glance as they strode away.

Between the stems of willow herb on the wasteground, two red eyes stared out at them as they passed.

They strode down Perivale's streets, streets that seemed eerily empty. Only the distant sound of sport and cartoons on several thousand televisions hinted at the location of the inhabitants of this seeming ghost town.

The Doctor paused to read a fading headline on a

15

torn and flapping sheet of paper on a newsagent's billboard.

LOCAL WOMEN STILL MISSING
POLICE ABANDON HOPE

He increased his pace to catch up with Ace. She was still stamping along the pavement, muttering to herself as she looked around her former home.

'Dead, all dead. We were the only life there ever was around here.'

Ace stopped so abruptly that the Doctor nearly cannoned into her back. She was staring at a pub, one which had been recently done up on the cheap: its sign was blazoned with chunky, plastic letters and hung above a door which swung open to reveal a glimpse of yards of fake, red leather, plastic plants and the insistent bleeping of electronic games machines.

For the first time since her arrival Ace's face thawed into her own uniquely mischievous grin.

'We used to come round here sometimes, hang about outside and try to get the big kids to buy us cans. Well, we're the big kids now aren't we?'

She jerked her thumb at the pub. 'That'll be where they are right? We're all nearly legal now, think of that Professor. Back in a sec.'

Ace vanished into the bar.

The Doctor hesitated. He looked at the pub and then at the building next door, a mini-market with piles of cans and special offers in the window. Seeming to have come to a decision he moved purposefully into the shop.

Inside he paused to stare at the rows of food and washing powder. He knew there was a procedure to be followed to get the goods he wanted, but what was it? He picked up a wire basket and examined its

16

construction, all the time looking for clues as he racked his memory. He had more absorbing issues occupying his intelligence than the rituals for exchanging goods on twentieth century Earth but he must have seen this a hundred times. What was it you did again?

A slight cough made him turn.

Two men who were leaning on either side of the counter at the other end of the shop watched him; each had the same morose stare. The one leaning on the till looked at the one leaning on the customers' side of the counter and shook his head.

'I don't know, Len.'

His friend pulled at the moustache that drooped mournfully over his mouth.

'Beats me, Harvey.'

The Doctor decided to ignore them. He began to move along a line of tins, scanning them for what he wanted. At the other end of the shop the conversation lumbered on again.

'Well, you take this Sunday opening.'

It was Harvey who spoke. Len provided an accompaniment of grunts of agreement, filtered through his moustache.

'Think I want to do it? Think I want to give up my one day of rest and come in here and sit in front of a cash register? Does your back in working at a till all day. It's a fact – there was a thing about it on the news the other night.'

Tinned peaches, tinned mandarins, tinned pineapple chunks, tinned rice pudding, tinned custard – the Doctor carefully scanned each shelf but he couldn't see what he wanted. Tinned sausages, tinned fish, tinned beans, tomatoes, sweet-corn and . . . there it was: tinned cat food in twelve or more varieties. The

Doctor scooped up a handful of cans and began to study their labels.

'Well, it's the law of the jungle though, right? Survival of the fittest.' Harvey's complaint continued. 'All these other shops, they're open aren't they? Where d'you think I'd be if I didn't join in? Down the plughole that's where, down the plughole without a paddle . . . CAN I HELP YOU?'

The last part of the sentence was seamlessly joined to the rest of it but bellowed down the shop at twice the volume. The Doctor jumped; a couple of cans dropped from the heap he was clutching and rolled towards the counter.

'Em . . . Yes, I think so.' The Doctor turned towards the two men. 'Which would you say they preferred?' He offered them a handful of tins of cat food.

Harvey and Len looked at each other. They looked back at the Doctor.

'What?' Harvey's response was as blank as his expression.

'Of these brands, which would you say our feline friends found particularly irresistible?'

Harvey and Len looked at each other again. Their worst fears about the Doctor's mental condition seemed to have been realized.

After a moment, Harvey cleared his throat. 'Well, if we are to believe the advertising, *that* one . . .' he pointed to the can the Doctor was holding in his right hand, '. . . is beloved of cat connoisseurs, and that one is the taste all cat-owners who really care put in the dish. He pointed at the cans still on the shelf. 'Whereas that one . . .' he pointed at the can that had rolled to the foot of the counter, '. . . has the smell that drives tabby cats wild.'

18

Len shook his head.

'Nah, that's an aftershave ad.'

'Is it?' Harvey was surprised.

Len pulled thoughtfully at his moustache. 'Or is it for cars?'

Harvey abandoned speculation and turned to the Doctor. He was still clutching the tins, looking at the two men enquiringly.

'Well, all I know is our Tiger goes mad for cheese.'

'Cheese . . . Thank you.'

The Doctor unceremoniously piled the tins he was holding back on the shelf and headed for the refrigerated cabinet.

Harvey looked at Len and rolled his eyes.

'Well, it's like I was saying Len,' he continued, returning to the business of the moment. 'It's the law of the jungle.'

Len leaned further over the counter and widened his eyes to emphasize what he was saying.

'These two guys, in a tent, in the jungle . . .'

Harvey broke into a slow grin.

'All right, all right, you got another one for me have you?' He settled himself behind the till and prepared to enjoy himself.

Len continued, 'So its dark, right, then they hear this terrible noise outside the tent – this terrible roaring . . .'

Red eyes watched from under the shelves. Furry belly flat to the dusty floor, the cat stared up and scented its quarry.

'. . . and the one guy turns to the other and he says, "Do you hear that? That's a lion".'

The Doctor felt a familiar prickling at the back of his neck, an instinctive warning that something lethal

19

was about to launch itself between his shoulder blades. He turned.

'So the other guy doesn't say a word, he just starts pulling on these running shoes, right?'

The Doctor began to move forward. He could see it, a faint dark shadow under the shelves. He took a tighter grip on his armful of cat food and cheese.

'And the first guy says, "What you doing? You can't run faster than a lion!" And the guy looks down at his running shoes and back at the other guy who's sitting there in his bare feet and he gives this really evil grin and says, "I don't have to outrun the lion."'

Two red eyes shot towards the Doctor's face. A dark thunderbolt of fur and muscle hurled itself at him with a low growling yowl. The Doctor yelled and ducked. He felt the draught of unsheathed claws sweeping past his face.

Then it was away. The door crashed to behind it and hung quivering on its hinges.

The Doctor tentatively straightened up.

Harvey and Len were gaping at him, mouths open in identical expressions of amazement. Eventually, Len swallowed and turned to Harvey.

'I told you, you should get that cat done.'

Harvey shook his head. 'That wasn't Tiger. I'm telling you, you put a catflap in and you get just anything coming into your house.'

The Doctor took a tight grip on his goods and left the shop. He was thinking furiously. Most of his thoughts concerned the probabilities of what he sensed was the horrible truth being the horrible truth. With another part of his brain he was already planning strategies to deal with that nightmare if it emerged. He had little attention left to do more than notice Ace sitting morosely on the kerb waiting for him and to realize there was no time to deal with her depression. He made a distracted effort.

'Did you find your friends?'

Ace looked up at him.

'No one even remembers them.'

The Doctor's attention was distracted again by his armload of groceries.

'I'm sure I've forgotten something,' he muttered.

'Oi!'

The Doctor turned to see Harvey glowering at him from the doorway of the shop.

'Haven't you forgotten something?' enquired Harvey with heavy politeness.

The Doctor beamed hopefully. 'Yes?'

'Money.'

The Doctor's face clouded. 'No that wasn't it.'

Ace looked at the cat food and lurid orange cheese that the Doctor was clutching.

'What do you want that lot for?'

'Hmm?'

The Doctor was evidently pondering some problem. Ace sighed and stood up, unloading handfuls of ten pence pieces from her pockets and counting them into Harvey's outstretched palm.

The Doctor frowned enquiringly at the heap of money. Ace shrugged.

'I got lucky on the fruit machine.

The Doctor looked sceptical.

'Lucky?'

Ace shrugged again.

'They're all fixed anyway, those machines.'

She wandered listlessly away up the street. The Doctor followed. He could think as he walked and he had a lot to think about.

Harvey shook his head as he watched them go. He moved back into the shop.

'I don't know, Len.'

He bent painfully to pick up the cans that were scattered over the floor.

'Beats me, Harvey,' replied Len.

Harvey froze. He stared under the shelf from which the strange animal had erupted. There was still something there, a furry, bloody remnant.

'Len . . .' He raised a face that was white with shock to look at his friend. 'I think something's eaten Tiger.'

Dark blood; dark fur; dark thoughts: the kitling followed the scent it had been guided to, but it was getting bored with that. There was a flash of movement as two children ran past its hiding place. It turned its head and sniffed at their warm, animal smell; the scent was closer and rawer than the one it had been ordered to pursue. It turned to follow this game, its stomach rumbling as low as the growling purr in its throat. It could sense the impatience of the hunter who guided it. The eyes that watched through the animal's were uninterested in the movement and the smell of meat.

The kitling didn't care. It was hungry; it needed a new game; it needed fresh quarry. It slunk out of its hiding place, eyes fixed on the two toddlers. A group of young mothers dawdled behind them with push-chairs. Across the road three older children moved in to monopolize the ball and improvise a game of football.

'Wait!'

The command checked the kitling. It paused, its

22

tail flicking all the while, and gave its purring growl again.

'Very well, very well, I will find you hunting but not here! You will be discovered.'

The kitling didn't concern itself with that either but the command was insistent. Grudgingly it slipped back into hiding.

None of the shops in Perivale's nearest precinct were open that Sunday. A few kids rattled down its concrete ramps on skateboards, their yells and whoops trailing after them as they vanished round the corner of a supermarket. Partial lighting in the shops showed mannequins standing motionless, arms outstretched to attract the attention of no one at all. The last receding whoop of the skateboarders echoed and died. An abandoned drinks can rocked on the ground where they had dropped it and then settled. There was silence.

Ace and the Doctor paused in the centre of the precinct. Ace leaned on the iron railing and stared down at the shops on the level below. Cheated of the distraction of following her, the Doctor began to walk in a small circle while staring intently at the ground. Were they actually the animals he feared and if so were they alone? How probable was that?

Ace looked at him and sighed. She opened her mouth to speak then paused, frowning.

Somewhere round the corner of the precinct a slow rattling trickled through the silence. Ace moved off to investigate. Still staring at the ground, the Doctor drifted after her.

Ace looked round and through the glass window of a chemist's shop and into the next courtyard of the

23

precinct. She peered through the shampoo bottles and shower caps and saw a young woman standing there dejectedly shaking a collecting can with monotonous jerks of her wrist. Her eyes were unfocused and stared ahead of her. The tip of her nose was bright red; between each jerk of her can she sniffed wetly. She wore a giant duffel coat, a hat that looked like a refugee from a wedding party of 1957, and Dr Martens.

Ace gaped at her and then shrieked, 'ANGE!'

She shot across the courtyard at the startled girl. Muttering now, the Doctor followed.

Ange took a tighter grip on her can, prominently labelled 'Hunt Saboteurs', as Ace careered towards her. Then, as the other girl skidded to a halt in front of her, beaming, Ange narrowed her eyes in recognition. She managed a watery grin.

'Hi, Ace, thought you were dead.'

Ace frowned. 'What?'

Ange sniffed. 'That's what they said: either you were dead or you'd gone to Birmingham,' she sniffed again. 'Comes to the same thing I suppose.'

The Doctor reached the two young women. He was no longer muttering. He was staring fixedly into the shop window behind Ange as if he had just seen something armed and dangerous. Ange glanced round nervously: a cluster of mannequins smiled plastic smiles, their stiff bodies softened by the fur coats that were draped over their shoulders – shining brown fur, white fur, yellow-striped and spotted fur, the Doctor gazed at the latter as if in shock.

Ange spoke out of the corner of her mouth.

'Who's he?'

Ace looked at the Doctor. His hat sat on the back of his head and he was pulling his trailing paisley scarf

24

agitatedly through his hands. She decided against a detailed explanation.

'He's just a friend of mine.'

'Oh.'

This answer seemed to satisfy Ange who turned to more pressing concerns.

'So, you're back to see your family?'

Ace shook her head curtly.

'So what are you doing here then?' Ange was bewildered. 'You're well out of this dump.'

Ace shrugged.

'I wanted to see my mates, didn't I. Catch up a bit.'

Ange sniffed again.

'Oh.'

The Doctor pressed closer to the glass. Yellow fur, spotted fur, hung limp and soft on the dummy like the dead thing it was. There was no hint of the long muscles that had animated it, the bone, sinew, heart and lungs of the animal that had worn it as its own skin as it streaked across the dusty yellow savannah, the fastest creature on earth. There was only the barest reminder of the coat's original owner, the animal that now reminded the Doctor so forcibly of the connection he had been looking for.

'But where are they coming from?' he muttered.

'Where is everyone?' Ace was almost pleading.

Ange sniffed. 'Who?'

Ace mentally searched through a host of names. She selected the first one at random.

'Jay?'

Ange shrugged. 'Dunno, moved over west someplace. Think he's doing window cleaning, that's what I heard.'

Ace waved her hands, looking for more names.

'Stevie?'

25

'Oh, he's gone.'

'Flo?'

'Married Darth.'

Ace was dumbstruck. 'Darth Vader, the brain-dead plumber? Flo?'

Ange nodded gloomily. 'Yeah, makes you think, eh?'

Ace was getting desperate. 'What about Shreela?'

Shreela had been one of her best friends, an apparently quiet girl with a wicked sense of humour that Ace had been one of the few privileged people to share.

Ange shook her head dismissively. 'Oh, she's gone.'

'Midge then?' She didn't even like Midge but still . . .

Another shake of the head. 'He's gone too.'

'What do you mean, gone? Gone where?'

Ange sniffed. 'I dunno. Gone. Vanished.'

'People don't just vanish!'

Ange looked at her sideways. 'You did.'

Ace shook herself nervously, 'Yeah, well, that's different.'

Ange looked at her sideways again. 'Is it?'

Ace opened her mouth to retort indignantly that being swept out of the chemistry lab by a time storm, hurled across the universe and subsequently involved in a whole series of adventures across time and space was hardly the same as moving up west to be a window cleaner. She closed her mouth and decided to stick to establishing the facts.

'Well when did they go?'

Ange scrubbed at her nose with the sleeve of her duffel coat. 'I dunno. Last month?'

'What! All of them?'

Ange considered. 'Well, Midge and Stevie went last

26

month; Shreela went last week. They had to scrape her mum off the ceiling. Funny, I always thought she got on all right with her family.

Shreela did get on with her family, Ace remembered, and Stevie had been planning to join his brother in a mini-cab firm. And Midge . . . Midge didn't have the imagination to leave Perivale. Ace shook her head.

'It doesn't make sense.'

'That's what I said. Know what I reckon?' Ange looked round her conspiratorily before moving closer to Ace. 'UFOs – they whisk them off and do experiments on them, like we do on animals. I wouldn't fancy cutting Stevie open to see what's inside would you?'

Ace didn't respond.

Ange raised her tin and rattled it under Ace's nose. 'Come on, give us ten pence at least.'

The Doctor turned away from the shop window. Ange hopefully raised her can to him. He stared at it blankly for a few seconds then scrabbled in his pocket and produced what appeared to be a thick, gold octagon. He peered at it dubiously for a second then attempted to shove it into the collecting tin. It stuck. The Doctor raised one finger and tapped it sharply. With a dull clunk several ounces of solid gold – one of the commonest metals on Psion B – added their weight to the cause of Hunt Saboteurs. The Doctor studied the can's label.

'It isn't a very efficient kind of hunt really when you think about it is it? All that noise and pantomime to slaughter one little animal,' he murmured.

Ange glanced at Ace for explanations of this weird little man. Ace didn't have any.

The Doctor continued, 'If you were going to hunt,

27

really hunt, you'd do it alone. You'd study your prey, observe its movements so you could surprise it alone and unsuspecting. And you wouldn't kill too many; you'd be very careful to cover your tracks so you could keep on hunting the same ground, so your prey would never even catch a smell of you.'

The Doctor turned his head sharply and sniffed energetically. 'Do you smell that?'

Ange attempted to inhale. 'I can't – hayfever. It's most likely glue, though.'

Ace looked at the Doctor suspiciously. 'What are you talking about, Professor? Is something going on here?'

The Doctor shook his head, still sniffing the air. 'I don't know, I'm not certain . . . yet.'

Ange glanced nervously at Ace. 'Is he . . . ?' she whispered, not even voicing what the Doctor might be, of which the least dangerous possibility was drunk.

Ace impatiently shook her head. When was the Doctor going to snap out of this? She tugged irritably at his sleeve. 'Professor, wake up will you!'

The Doctor turned on her and asked, 'When is a cat not a cat?' An enquiring finger punctuated the question, jabbing under Ace's nose. She looked blank. The Doctor smiled. 'When it builds its own catflap.'

He produced a tin of cat food from his pocket and waved it at her.

'Bait. Come on Ace.'

He turned on his heel and began to stride out of the precinct.

Ace gaped at his retreating back. 'Hang on, Professor!' She sprinted after him.

Ange watched them go. She shrugged, sniffed and rattled her can. At least that was heavier than it had been.

* * *

On the other side of the door, the hunter sat watching. Its eyes were dark and ancient; as it watched they changed. The irises glowed yellow and the pupils narrowed to slits. They were cat's eyes.

The voice whispered, 'Show me.'

Across the gulf that the door opened on to, the kitling saw. It crouched at the base of a wall and stared up with its red eyes at the man jogging past.

The jogger was Stuart. He pounded down the empty road punching the air, dancing on his toes and giving little, whistling breaths. The man and the cat were the only living things in sight.

On the other side of the door the hunter saw and smiled.

'Yes,' it whispered. 'Yes, he will do very well.'

It gave the signal that let the animals loose, leaping down on to the world where the kitling waited for its share of the game.

Chapter 3

Stuart was jogging with his head down, but he looked up when he heard the sound of hoofbeats ahead of him. He froze with terror, then turned and pelted in the other direction. Behind him the hoofbeats grew louder; his pursuer was gaining easily. Stuart tried to stretch his legs further; sobbing, he tried to dodge. A door opened in the air in front of him and Stuart toppled through, screaming.

On the wall the kitling looked again at the empty street. It rose, stretched its long claws and got ready to jump in its turn.

Ace and the Doctor came round the corner of the road. The kitling paused. The hunter's command rang in its brain: 'Wait, watch them!'

The kitling hesitated, torn between its hunger and its instructions.

Ace was talking agitatedly. As she waved her arms, the many badges on her jacket flashed in the sun. The kitling, its head on one side, considered the movement. It jumped down behind the wall and slipped into the bushes. It could watch from hiding. Ace and the Doctor drew level with the wall. They stopped, Ace still talking angrily.

'Can't believe he said that you know, that plod, I reckon that was well out of order. Ten pence? I mean even if I could've phoned, which I couldn't, right? Do you think they'd have listened?'

The Doctor looked around the street: it was deserted and near what he suspected was the main area of activity. He nodded in satisfaction and began to unburden his pockets of cat food and cheese, laying them in a row on top of the wall.

Ace struggled on. 'I mean it's not that I don't . . . well, mum and me . . . oh, you know Professor.' She was thinking of her last visit to Earth: it had been 1945 and she had seen her mother. But then her mother was a helpless baby that Ace had come to love without even knowing who she was.

It had been a strange and disturbing insight into her relationship to her parents, but now she was back in her own time it seemed to have no more to do with her present feelings for them than a picture of a baby.

All in all, Ace was more confused than she wanted to be or knew how to deal with. And the Doctor didn't even appear to be listening to her. He held a tin of cat food and was apparently trying to remember something. He frowned in exasperation. 'Tin-opener!' he muttered. He knew he had forgotten something.

Ace tried again. 'Well, when I asked you to bring me here . . . It's not like I was homesick for a place, just that time – just the whole crowd. We had a really good laugh you know. I can't believe they've all just disappeared.'

The Doctor looked at her at last. He held out his hand. 'Tin-opener, Ace,' he said with the tone of a

31

surgeon demanding a vital piece of equipment from their nurse.

Ace stared at him for a moment before reaching into her pocket. She brought out a Swiss army knife. She opened the appropriate blade and handed the knife to him. Her face was expressionless; her voice struggled to conceal the aching lump that had just appeared in her throat. 'Professor, are you listening to me?'

The Doctor licked one finger and raised it in the air to check the direction of the wind. He didn't look at her. 'Shhh! Ace, I'm concentrating.'

For a numb and disbelieving moment Ace went on staring at him. She swallowed hard, pushed herself off the wall and began to walk away. She looked back once.

The Doctor had placed a row of opened tins at the base of the wall. He hesitated, took a lump of cheese and laid that down as well. He didn't look round.

Ace turned swiftly on her heel. With her head down and shoulders hunched, she walked quickly away.

The Doctor didn't notice. He checked his arrangements again and nodded in satisfaction. He climbed over the wall and crouched in the garden on the other side. Only his hat and eyes were visible as he peered over the top of the wall at the opened cans.

The kitling followed the woman wearing the bright badges as it had been instructed.

Ace slowed her pace as soon as the Doctor was out of sight. The streets were empty; she had nowhere to go. She stopped next to a children's playground. Three swings hung on one chain only; a fourth was still intact. Ace wandered over and sat down. She swung herself gently to and fro staring into space.

There was no one left here that she knew or wanted to see: no one to witness the changes in her; no one to reassure her that she had grown up but her childhood was intact.

Ace sighed. She wished she had never come back. She wished she could leave, but she could not think of anywhere she wanted to go.

A plaintive mew sounded from near her feet. Ace looked down to see a large cat twining itself round her ankles. Ace gave a half smile.

'Come on then,' she said as she picked up the cat. Her eyes widened in surprise: it was a lot larger and heavier than she had thought. She heaved it into her lap and began to stroke it.

The cat purred a deep powerful purr and blinked its red eyes.

Mrs Bates at number thirty-three was having a trying day. First there had been that terrible cat-fight in the herbaceous border – she still hadn't been able to bring herself to investigate the results of that – and now she had a strange man crouching in front of her rose bushes. She tapped on the glass of the window.

The Doctor was holding his breath as a small cat slunk up to his bait.

'Pssst!' he hissed at it.

The cat raised its head startled. Its eyes were greeny-yellow, the wide alarmed eyes of a domestic tabby.

The Doctor sighed in disappointment. He became aware of an insistent rapping behind him. He turned and saw the elderly woman mouthing something at him through the glass. He flapped his hand at her.

'Shhh!' He turned back to his trap.

The tabby sniffed the nearest tin of cat food and

backed off, sneezing. The Doctor frowned, reached down and replaced that tin with a piece of cheese.

Mrs Bates had had enough. She was calling the police.

Ace had considered her options and realized she had none. If it was a choice between life back in Perivale without even the company of her friends or another three years of her time in the TARDIS she would stick with the Doctor, at least until he took her somewhere she wanted to be. She wanted to be somewhere she could feel she belonged – really belonged – somewhere where people wanted her. She could not even imagine the place.

Suddenly impatient she stood up. The cat slid out of her lap.

'Sorry, mogs,' muttered Ace. She started to walk back the way she had come.

The kitling watched her go.

Ace had walked only a few yards when she felt the faintest stirring of the hairs on the back of her neck. Her body, long trained to danger, had sensed something behind her. She turned to face it.

It was sitting on a horse: a tall black horse draped as if for a medieval joust. Its shape was humanoid but the hands that clutched the horse's mane had only three, long, jointed fingers tipped by lethal-looking claws. It was covered in smooth yellow spotted fur and its head was the head of a great cat: a cheetah. It glinted against the grey background of Perivale. It was beautiful.

Ace was awed. 'Wow!'

The Cheetah Person smiled. Only its mouth moved to reveal a collection of gleaming, pointed teeth; its yellow eyes with their narrow black pupils burned

34

into Ace. Ace realized she was in very serious trouble. She ran.

The hoofbeats were almost instantly on top of her; she could hear the horse snorting just behind her head. The Cheetah Person made no sound. Ace ducked behind the swings in an attempt to keep them between her and the horse.

The Cheetah Person checked its mount. It stared through the chains of the swings at her and smiled again. A narrow, pink tongue licked its whiskers in anticipation.

Ace gulped. Once again she had no options left. 'Doctor help! HELP!'

The Doctor watched with some irritation as a Yorkshire terrier came sniffing round his tins. 'Shoo!' he flapped at it angrily.

The dog ignored him and started to tuck into a tin of pilchard surprise.

'Go away!' The Doctor flapped more vigorously. It was then that he heard distant hoofbeats and Ace's voice.

'Doctor, help!'

He hadn't even noticed her leave. He vaulted over the wall and began to run at full speed in the direction of her cries.

Ace hadn't been able to dodge around the swings for long. The Cheetah Person rode bareback but seemed able to manoeuvre its mount with the speed of its thought. It had cut her off and flushed her out. It seemed to be playing with her: it pursued her until, out of breath, she stumbled; it then circled her as she panted and waited until Ace tried to break past before chasing her again.

All the while its lean muscles tensed beneath its gleaming, smooth fur, its long claws gripped the horse's mane with an expert touch and it smiled, baring all those white needle-points of teeth.

Ace had stopped dead. Exhausted, she glared up at it. She had had enough.

The Cheetah Person seemed to understand that the game was over. It paused for a moment and then kicked its horse straight at Ace with a new purpose.

Ace couldn't control the instinct that made her duck and run one last time, or the scream that burst from her throat as the claws raked at her hair. The air opened into a door in front of her and she fell headlong through it.

When the Doctor came panting round the corner only the gently moving swings showed that anyone had been there at all.

Ace was still running as she came through the door. It took a few seconds for her to check and try to comprehend what had happened to her. There had been a sensation of the air itself parting in front of her, of falling into blackness beyond and now . . .

It was a desert landscape. Pale, yellow, sunbaked earth stretched ahead of her. Tall grasses bleached by the sun and a few clumps of black, thorny trees like ink sketches stood out against the pale land. On the horizon, smoke trickled into the pale sky from the pointed tops of the mountains. The area was a desert ringed with volcanoes.

Ace was shaking. It was as if she had come from a dream into full consciousness but couldn't believe she was awake. There was movement in the grass beside her. She looked round.

A group of kitlings regarded her with red eyes

36

before returning to their meal. Their powerful, dark bodies wandered lazily over the mound they were dismembering. It was a body. Its hand was visible between the feeding backs of the kitlings: the hand clutched a pink sponge that was last used on the windscreen of a car.

Ace took a tentative step towards the body but turned when she heard the soft sound of hooves on the grass behind her.

The Cheetah Person had appeared out of the air behind her. It sat poised on its horse, watching her with bright yellow eyes.

Ace looked round frantically: there was nowhere to hide. She ran.

The kitling was very hungry now, but the commands of the hunter echoed in its brain: 'Wait! Wait! Hunt the other one! Bring me the other one!'

The kitling wasn't inclined to obey but its instructions had never been this insistent before. It shook its head and made low, disgruntled yowls. It wanted to leap through the door in its turn; it wanted to feed. Then it smelled food. Ignoring the commands that resounded in its head, it turned and trotted towards the scent.

The Doctor walked back towards his bait. He was thinking furiously. He knew where Ace had gone – where she had been taken. He knew he had very little time to reach her. And could predict with horrible accuracy what was probably happening to her. But he could not get to her until . . .

The Doctor froze. There, gnawing at the cheese he had left out on the pavement, was a large black cat. It raised its head and stared at him. It had red eyes.

'Got you!' he whispered.

'Got you!' It wasn't an echo, it was Sergeant Paterson. A heavy hand fell on the Doctor's shoulder.

The kitling bolted.

Paterson tightened his grip as the Doctor tried to struggle free. 'Now then, what do you think you're up to? I've had complaints. Neighbourhood Watch – they've been keeping an eye on you.'

The Doctor thrashed against the blue serge arms that were locked around him. 'Look, there's no time. I have to follow that cat!'

Paterson shook his head. 'You're a public nuisance.'

The Doctor made one last attempt. 'Will you let go of me!'

'Now don't be stupid, eh? Don't get yourself into real trouble.' Paterson was almost smiling, confident in his ability to pin the small man down.

The Doctor stopped struggling. He twisted to look into Paterson's face.

'One finger can be a deadly weapon?'

He tapped Paterson gently in the centre of the forehead with his index finger. Paterson dropped as if he had been poleaxed.

The Doctor dusted his hands and began to jog up the street in pursuit of the kitling. There was nothing that anyone could teach him about self-defence.

Ace had no breath left but she kept running. Her legs had no strength: they wobbled wildly and sent her crashing into the rocks. She fell.

She could hear the horse behind her, just trotting. She looked round.

The Cheetah Person rode past her and stopped. It leisurely dismounted and began to move towards her in a half crouch. Its eyes blazed and a low, purring growl came from its throat.

38

Ace looked for a weapon. She had fallen near a clump of blackened trees. Her eye caught a movement at the edge of the bushes.

A dirty, bloodstained face peered out at her. It looked terrified. It was Stuart, the boy she had last seen wrestling in Paterson's self-defence class. He hissed at Ace and stared past her at the approaching Cheetah Person.

'Go away! Get away from here!' he shouted.

Ace looked back at the Cheetah Person. It had paused to listen and to sniff the air. It turned its head towards Stuart and gave its purring growl.

Stuart gave a sob of terror and stumbled out of the trees, looking frantically for somewhere to escape to or where he could hide.

Ace dragged herself to her feet, grabbing at a rock. The Cheetah Person glided towards them in a crouching lope.

Stuart ran. The Cheetah Person sprang after him in a sudden flash of speed. Ace raised her rock to strike but it sped past her and almost knocked her over. In seconds it was on Stuart's back, attacking him in a flurry of claws and teeth. Stuart gave three high, desperate screams and fell silent.

Ace swallowed. She shook as she raised her rock again and began to stumble towards the Cheetah Person. Her breath came quickly.

The Cheetah Person rose and wiped a paw over its muzzle. It bent and easily heaved Stuart's body over its shoulder. It began to walk back towards its horse but it stopped when it saw Ace.

Ace looked into the creature's wild, yellow eyes. The Cheetah Person bared its teeth in a threatening smile. Ace stepped back.

Ignoring her, the Cheetah Person threw Stuart's body over its horse, mounted and galloped off.

As Ace watched it ride away she saw a young woman emerge from the edge of the trees. Her face was gaunt; her clothes were in rags. She looked blankly at Ace.

'He shouldn't have run,' she said dully. 'They always go for you if you run.'

Ace gaped at her in disbelief. 'Shreela!' she called.

Shreela gave a faint, weary smile. 'Hi, Ace.'

The Doctor was hot on the kitling's trail. He had it cornered behind a pile of dustbins. He dropped to a crouch and began to stalk it, peering past the bins to catch a glimpse of the animal's baleful red eyes.

'Why don't you come out and we'll talk about this sensibly, hmmm?' He reached out to the animal.

The dustbins went flying as the kitling burst out and streaked up the alley. The Doctor pounded after it.

At the other end of the lane, Paterson saw his attacker disappearing, one hand clutching his hat to his head. Paterson's mouth tightened. He would soon see who had the best moves in a fair fight. He ran after them.

Shreela led Ace through the trees, ducking under the low thorny branches. She didn't speak. Ace looked at Shreela's thin, scratched arms and battered, bleeding feet and swallowed her questions.

They emerged into a small clearing in the centre of which a tiny fire smoked fitfully. Two boys were bent over the fire: one held a stick with the skinned body of some kind of scraggy rodent over the smoke; the other chewed on some leaves with no apparent appetite. This second boy was shaking and muttering to himself. Both of them wore the grubby remnants of jeans and T-shirts. They were grey; their eyes stared out from sunken sockets. They looked at Ace without curiosity.

'Midge?' Ace couldn't believe it was him. He was like a ghost of the boy she had known.

He stared at her, still chewing a bitter mouthful of leaves.

'Hi Ace, long time . . .'

Ace looked round. 'Is Stevie here too?'

Shreela spoke quietly beside her. 'He was.'

Midge spat. 'Stevie? He's cat food isn't he?'

The other boy began to laugh wildly.

Shreela turned on him. 'Stop it!'

The boy stopped laughing abruptly. Midge nodded at him. 'This is Derek. He's doing really well – been here three weeks and has only flesh wounds.'

Derek grinned at Ace. He was shaking violently. Midge turned away and seemed to lose interest in the conversation.

Ace looked from him to Shreela. These were her friends, her gang. They were aged, desperate and defeated after being dragged across the universe to feed these lethal hunters.

Shreela dropped her eyes. 'We'll have to move on soon: they sometimes hunt at night.'

Midge stared into space, rocking himself. 'They can see in the dark. You can't see them, just their eyes.'

Ace took a deep breath. She stepped into the centre of their circle and looked at them all challengingly. She, at least, was not going to go under so soon. 'Just as well I'm back, you need sorting out, you lot.'

★　★　★

41

The Doctor was closing on the kitling. It seemed to be waiting for him, poised on the top of a high wall. The kitling's tail flicked as the animal watched the Doctor run towards it.

As he ran he knew this must be a trap, but it was his only way through. It was the only way to reach Ace.

He sprang up the wall.

As he leapt he felt a hand close on his ankle. Paterson's voice bellowed in triumph. 'Oh no you don't!'

'Paterson, you fool, let go!'

It was too late. The kitling leapt. The air opened and Paterson and the Doctor toppled into another world.

It was hot. The sun blazed down on them and bounced off the pale earth around them. They lay on bleached grass staring into the unblinking yellow eyes of a herd of animals. Cheetah People sprawled round them and chewed on raw meat or basked in the midday glare. The Doctor looked at the lithe, furry humanoids and knew they were the hunters he had suspected as being behind this. He had heard of but never seen them: they were as beautiful as the descriptions he had been given. He watched in admiration as the closest animal yawned, showing off its delicate gleaming teeth. Paterson lay prone, taking shocked, whistling breaths as he looked round wildly.

The Doctor sat up carefully and took a better look around. A few skin tents were scattered on the flat yellow plain. The Cheetah People's horses stood tethered and grazing beside them. Volcanoes smoked lazily on the horizon. The Doctor stood up slowly. He was looking for something else – someone else –

because someone had directed the savage instincts of these animals to bring him here.

The kitling he had chased was trotting away from him across the grass. It moved towards a group of Cheetah People that were sprawled in a cluster, chewing on bones and licking themselves. They parted to let it through, revealing the dark figure that sat enthroned on piles of furs among them.

With a prickling sense of foreboding, the Doctor stared into the dark eyes he recognized. The man in black with his smooth hair and neat beard seemed almost benign, but the Doctor knew him as his oldest and most familiar adversary. Suddenly he knew they were all in even greater danger than he had suspected.

'Why Doctor,' the Master smiled, 'what an unexpected pleasure.'

The Master's eyes became those of a cat; his smile was a toothy snarl.

Chapter 4

The Master stood up slowly. The Doctor watched as the yellow faded from his eyes as if it had never been there. The Master smiled the urbane smile of a host inviting his guests to join the party.

'Run, Doctor,' he coaxed.

The Doctor and Paterson looked round. The Cheetah People were closing in on them, whiskers quivering and pink tongues licking needle-sharp teeth. Paterson gave a gulp of terror and began to bolt.

The Doctor grabbed his shoulder. 'Don't move!' he commanded.

The Cheetah People hesitated in their advance. They looked from Paterson to the Doctor to the Master, sniffing at the air.

Without moving any other part of his body, the Master reached into his pocket and produced a small, shiny sphere. Suddenly he hurled it straight at Paterson. The Cheetah People followed the movement. They leapt snarling at the policeman. The ball bounced at Paterson's feet. He yelled and ran.

The Doctor tried to grab him. 'Paterson! No!'

He was too late. Paterson was surrounded by snarling

Cheetah People. They circled him and batted him with their gleaming claws.

The Master came to stand beside the Doctor, still smiling.

'I was relying on your intelligence, Doctor. It would be such an inelegant death.'

Together they watched as Paterson fell. The Cheetah People dropped back. One remained to prod at Paterson until he staggered up. The game resumed: the Cheetah People darted at him, batting him from one to the other. They let him try to run, tripped him, and then prodded him to his feet.

The Doctor was reminded of a domestic cat on Earth playing with a trapped animal.

The Master nodded as if he caught the thought. 'They are essentially a fun-loving species.' His tone became brisk. 'Now Doctor, there are things I must discuss with you.'

The Doctor refused to be distracted. Paterson was bleeding now. 'That was a good trick, with the ball,' he said casually.

The Master took three more of the spheres out of his pocket and admired them in the sunlight. 'Pretty aren't they? They are a . . . useful distraction.'

'Charming.' The Doctor's hand flashed out and snatched the balls from The Master. He ran straight at the Cheetah People who were closing in on Paterson again.

The Master made an angry movement after him then checked himself. 'No, Doctor! Come back!'

Paterson had fallen again. The Cheetahs moved in on him with hungry purrs, claws unsheathed. It was clear the game was about to end. The Doctor looked round rapidly. The Cheetahs and their prey were close

45

by one of the skin tents. An untethered horse grazed beside it.

'Psst!' the Doctor hissed, skidding to a halt in front of the animals.

In unison the Cheetahs turned to look at him. The Doctor began to juggle with the shining balls. The yellow eyes fixed on the movement; one of the Cheetahs reached out a paw to bat at a ball. The Doctor moved back a few paces to lead the animals away from Paterson who lay battered and breathless on the ground behind them. The Doctor abruptly caught the balls and hurled them away from him. The sun glinted on them as they whizzed off in three directions.

'Fetch!' commanded the Doctor.

Cold, yellow Cheetah eyes regarded him without emotion. Still moving as one, the Cheetahs took a prowling step towards the Doctor.

'Fetch?' he repeated with more doubt than hope.

'I'm afraid they will not be so easily distracted, Doctor.' The Master had come to stand behind the animals. 'They're hungry.'

The Cheetahs took another step.

'No!'

The animals turned to look at the Master.

'Come Doctor, why don't we leave these creatures to their meal.' The Master indicated Paterson who was staggering to his feet, wild-eyed and dishevelled.

The Doctor didn't even bother to reply. Glancing sideways he saw the grazing horse close by. He made a lunge at it and leapt on its back. The Cheetahs snarled and leapt at him.

'No!' The Master darted between the animals and the Doctor, holding up a commanding arm. The Cheetah People hesitated. 'I'm warning you, Doctor, I control these animals. Come back to me now!'

The Doctor reached down and helped Paterson heave himself on to the horse. 'Healthy exercise Paterson, it'll do you the world of good,' he murmured.

'I command them, Doctor. I can order them to eat you alive. Come back!' The Master was shouting furiously over his shoulder, still holding up one arm to check the Cheetah People.

The Doctor raised his hat in farewell, smiled politely and kicked the horse into a gallop.

The Master watched them recede. He slammed his fist into his other hand in frustration. A low growl brought his attention back to the animals around him. Burning yellow eyes considered him hungrily. The Cheetah People moved slowly to encircle him. The Master raised a commanding hand again, they stopped but did not back off. They growled again.

'Very well,' he said quietly. 'Very well, I will find some other hunting for you.'

Ace looked round the landscape. The heat bounced off the yellow ground at her but she shivered. It was not a world that offered comfort or shelter to anything human. She looked again at the smoking volcanoes on the horizon, across a dry plain speckled with twisted, black thorns. Close by was the half dried and dismembered carcass of some kind of antelope. Curling horns curved away from its skull. A kitling prowled over the body, feeding.

Ace was aware of Shreela coming to stand at her shoulder. She too looked at the kitling.

'They don't bother us,' she said. 'They only eat us when we're dead. It's like they're watching us though.'

Ace nodded. There were other skulls of various

47

sizes and shapes littered over the pale grass. She stared into their empty eye-sockets for a second before turning away. Midge and Derek were sitting disconsolately on the ground some distance away. She took a deep breath and looked round the three of them.

'OK, so what do we do?'

Midge gave her a scornful stare. 'Do?'

Derek began to shake and giggle, looking from Ace to Midge. Ace ignored him.

Midge got to his feet. He advanced on Ace, his cold hopeless stare adding a further chill to his words. 'We die,' he whispered. 'Maybe today, maybe next week. We could go and find one of the big pussy cats, hurry things along a bit. Is that what you want to try?'

He was face to face with Ace. He waited for her reply. There was none; he smiled mirthlessly.

'I tried to fight one once, it'd caught Stevie,' Shreela offered.

Midge threw her a contemptuous glance. 'She threw sticks at it, didn't she?'

'Oh, and where were you Midge?' Ace's voice was as low as his had been and her stare reflected his own contempt at him. Nose to nose they stared each other down.

Shreela moved closer to them. She touched Ace's arm. 'You can't hurt them Ace.'

'They're invincible.' Derek's voice startled the others. They turned to look at him. He was still shaking but the crazy smile had faded from his face. He stared back at them from sunken eye-sockets. He looked like a crumpled, little old man.

Ace saw he was nursing recent and ugly gashes to his arms, the marks of claws.

Ace shook herself mentally. The despair of her one-time friends was numbing her own resourceful brain

48

into defeatism. Whatever they were facing on this planet she knew she and the Doctor had seen and survived worse. She drew herself up. 'Nothing's invincible,' she said with quiet conviction.

Midge snorted. 'That's right, Ace: you tell us; you sort us out.'

Shreela was looking nervously round the empty plain. 'We better get back to the clearing. We're not safe here in the open.'

Ace was already scanning the landscape. She considered their options for survival and looked back at the copse of thorn they had emerged from.

'Are we safe there? At least out here we can see them coming.'

Shreela shook her head. 'They don't usually bother us in there. They only hunt in the open unless they're hungry – then they take us anywhere.'

Ace nodded. All right, she thought, work out their habits and you'll learn their weaknesses. 'Why do they only hunt out here?'

'What do you think this is, The Wonderful World of Wildlife?' Midge burst out. 'Who knows! Who cares! Why do they always ride up there to get their water?' he pointed to a nearby gully that was fringed with tall thorn trees. 'Why do they eat us without ketchup? Why do they bite your leg off one day and wait three more to finish you off?' he ranted.

Ace looked at him for a moment as he spat his sarcasm at her. She had a sudden vivid memory of her head connecting with the glass of the youth club door and the mocking laughter of Midge and his mates. 'Want to lose six pounds of ugly flesh, Ace? Cut your head off!' as they swung her through the air and into the door again.

She interrupted him abruptly.

49

'They always ride up there?' She pointed towards the gully he had indicated.

Midge shrugged. 'So what?'

Ace stared at him levelly. 'So let's get one.'

He looked at her for a minute and then started to laugh. 'Do what?'

'Nothing's invincible,' Ace looked round at Shreela and Derek. 'You've got to fight back.'

Shreela met her eyes. After a minute she nodded briefly.

Midge was still laughing. 'Yeah, we could dig a big hole and put twigs on top, eh? Get a big net and scoop them all up in that, right Ace?'

Ace didn't even look at him. She was staring at the gully and assessing it. She pulled some thin wire out of her pocket. 'What do you think this is, Midge? A Tarzan film?' She looked at the wire, tested its tension, and turned to Shreela. 'You got anything?'

Shreela looked at her seriously. She didn't move.

Ace watched her anxiously. She needed Shreela because she didn't have the energy to carry three of them through this, and one of them would die.

Shreela slowly reached into her pocket. She pulled out some strips of stiff, chewed leather. 'We could knot them together,' she offered quietly.

Ace grinned. Not only was Shreela still fighting back, she had already understood Ace's plan. She considered their pathetic heap of equipment. Wire and rags, she thought: they would have to do.

'OK, let's do it.'

Ace and Shreela began to walk determinedly up the gully. Ace looked back over her shoulder at Midge and Derek. 'Come on, make yourself useful can't you?'

The young men looked at each other and reluctantly trailed after the women.

The Doctor slowed his mount to a walk. There had been no pursuit. Glancing behind him he saw that they had put a line of low sandhills between themselves and the Cheetahs. The pale rock shone red now; above them the sky boiled with smoke. The sun burning sultrily through its billows.

It looked, the Doctor reflected, like a very young or a very ancient world. Planets, like people, began and ended in incoherence. On the horizon, lava bubbled. The sky itself seemed to be on fire. It could be that this planet was still forming itself, but the rocks – the rocks were ancient.

The Doctor became aware that Paterson was talking.

'That's just not like me you know. It's not, you ask anyone. Sarge'll keep his head in a crisis, you ask any of the lads. I don't scare easy, Doctor, believe you me.'

The Doctor glanced round at the other man. Paterson's eyes flicked round the alien landscape; his expression was hunted, dazed. Only his tone was still blustering.

'I was on one of those survival courses, SAS style of thing.'

The Doctor saw a kitling calmly sitting in their path. It looked as small and innocent as a domestic tabby. Only its red eyes betrayed its intelligence and its menace.

Paterson burbled on. 'Pitting your wits against the environment – raw survival. I was the only one that ate the worm stew, there's courage for you if you like.'

'Very impressive,' murmured the Doctor. He

51

slowed the horse, gazing intently back at the kitling. It was, he realized, in communication with him. He sensed its presence on the edge of his mind, a wild, raw power that clawed for admission. Without any certainty as to why the Doctor kept his mind firmly closed to it, this particular unknown smelled too dangerous. He would talk to any creature in the universe, but not until he knew whether it was armed and with what.

'But this is just . . . Where the hell are we anyway?' some of Paterson's agitation crept into his voice.

The Doctor looked round at him again. He knew he was looking at a man who was keeping a slender grasp on his sanity with no resources of imagination to fall back on. Paterson couldn't imagine anything like the events he had just lived through; he couldn't imagine anything like the place in which he now found himself. But here he was, staring it all in the face. The Doctor tried to break the worst to him carefully.

'We're on the planet of the Cheetah People. They're intelligent carnivores. No one knows much about them.' The Doctor hesitated before saying, 'No one's survived long enough to find out.'

Paterson fixed him with a glassy and ominously blank stare. 'You trying to tell me we're on another planet?' His voice, too, was horribly calm.

'Yes.' The Doctor waited for him to crack. Nothing happened. Slightly reassured he continued. 'It's very odd, I've never heard of the Cheetah People hunting away from their own feeding grounds before.'

They could leap from world to world but not into the unknown. They had no knowledge of Earth, nor even of that galaxy. Their prey was always on neighbouring worlds and they moved away from one only when they had run down and eaten everything that moved. Earth was light years outside their territory.

The kitling still watched him. Its message still throbbed unacknowledged at the edge of his consciousness. He met its red eyes again.

Kitlings – feline vultures – too had the power of teleportation and the intelligence and curiosity to let it take them right across the universe. They could smell blood even across the vacuum of space. They jumped from world to world looking for carrion. It was by following the kitlings that the Cheetahs found their hunting, but where the Cheetahs found sport enough they stopped; the kitlings roamed on, snacking off the destruction they smelled out. Sooner or later the kitlings would move in on any primitive culture that produced enough dead bodies. They had been on Earth before, many times, but this time the Doctor knew they had been controlled. That had to be the Master's doing, but for what purpose?

The kitling rose leisurely. It stretched, yawned and then strolled away.

On the horizon a great column of lava leapt from the nearest volcano. Its roar reached them seconds later. The Doctor frowned. It could be that the planet was still young and unstable, but the rocks were etched by aeons of the planet's hot winds and that the rocks on the horizon were breaking up.

'We may be in very serious trouble Paterson, very serious,' said the Doctor.

Paterson cleared his throat. 'You're the one that's on another planet, aren't you, eh?' His bluster grew more confident. 'You better let me look after things, Doc, best way.'

The Doctor sighed. 'Do you have any idea where we are?'

Paterson threw a hunted look around the landscape. 'I'll soon get my bearings once I've worked out the wind direction and angle of the sun.'

The Doctor shook his head sadly. As he had surmised, the policeman's mind had just toppled quietly over the edge. He kicked the horse forward.

'Hey!' Paterson lurched behind him, nearly losing his grip. 'Eh, don't you think I should drive, Doc?'

Two red eyes stared out through the rib-cage of a long-dead antelope and watched as the Doctor and Paterson rode away.

It was not easy to climb the thorn trees. Their black bark gave off an acrid powder as the young women gripped them which made the climbers sneeze and cough. The thorns jutted out of the branches like dark stilettos; their sharp points could rip flesh wide open. There was already a long gash in Ace's jacket.

Finally, each of the girls reached a crook in the branches of their respective trees. Each was perched on the opposite side of the narrow, stony gully. Ace had the thin wire uncoiled in her hands. Each end of the wire was weighted with strips of cloth and leather.

She threw one end across the gully at Shreela and then busied herself tying her end of the wire to the tree. When she looked across she saw that Shreela still held the cord slackly. She was staring anxiously down the gully.

'Come on Shreela!' Ace hissed.

Shreela waved an arm, signalling Ace to be quiet. Then Ace heard it too – approaching hoofbeats. Moving rapidly now, Shreela tied her end of the wire to the branches and pulled the line tight across the gully.

Ace squinted anxiously at the wire. When she

moved her head the light glinted on the wire, but she hoped the trap would be invisible from the ground. She had judged the height of the wire to catch a mounted Cheetah Person across the chest or neck. It ought at least to knock the creature off its horse. If the rider approached at speed they could hope to injure it badly, even kill it.

The sound of hoofbeats clattered up the gully now: the horse was moving fast. Ace ducked down as far as she could in the branches. There was little cover so she froze and hoped she would not be noticed. She buried her head in her arms; she had the superstitious feeling that the Cheetah would feel her eyes if she looked at it. The sound of the horse was loud she could hear it snorting . . .

There was silence.

Slowly Ace raised her head. Two blazing yellow eyes glared up at her. The Cheetah watched her for a long time until she felt herself begin to shake. It then turned a similar stare on Shreela who cowered in the branches opposite. Finally it urged its horse into a walk and began to move forward. Ace held her breath. It was almost on the wire.

The Cheetah raised its paw, unfolded its claws from the pad of its paw like a set of flick-knives and sliced through the wire. The Cheetah rode on without even checking its mount. Urging its horse into a trot, the creature clattered away from them. It did not look back.

Ace pulled up her half of the wire and examined the end. The fine steel had been sliced without even bending the wire. It was a clean break. She looked up at Shreela.

To her amazement Shreela was giving her a wan but encouraging smile. 'Plan B?' suggested Shreela.

Ace grinned back. Shreela was right: they were not beaten yet.

The Master looked again into the yellow eyes around him. They had moved closer as he had brooded, stroking the kitling he held in his lap. The Cheetah People breathed their hunger. Hot breath exhaled from seven, panting red mouths. The Master knew he had to deal with them at once.

He raised the kitling in the air. Its soft fur brushed his face as he whispered into a large, dark ear, 'Go hunting.'

With an eager growl, the kitling dropped from his lap and sprang into the air. It vanished.

With cat's eyes that matched its own, the Master watched where the kitling had gone.

Ace worked rapidly, wrapping the last of her rags around the end of a branch. Beside her, Shreela worked on another. Ace reached into her pocket and checked again that her lighter was there; she drew it out and checked the flame. She went back to tying rags.

From under a neighbouring bush, Midge glared out at her. Ace had made them all crouch in the undergrowth once the new trap had been set. The young men had followed her, but offered no help now as Ace and Shreela worked to make crude torches. Midge curled his lip at her.

'Where'd you pick up this little scheme, Ace? The Girl Guides?'

Ace had once been a Brownie, an Imp. She never made it into the Guides. There had been a nasty incident at the summer camp involving Brown Owl and a makeshift Molotov cocktail: the fairy marquee had never been the same again. Ace was sure that Midge knew that as well as she did.

'This particular trap was devised by a guy I know. He was a commando in World War Two. They used it very effectively in a raid into occupied France in 1942.' She went on knotting rags. 'He told me about it himself.' Last week, she added to herself, in 1943.

Midge was no longer listening. He was staring at Derek. Ace followed the direction of his gaze. Derek had begun to drool, his eyes were unfocused and he was rocking himself backwards and forwards. He cradled his wounds and hummed to himself.

'He'll get us all killed!' Midge shot out a backhanded slap with all his weight behind it. Derek fell back clutching his bleeding mouth. Ace grabbed Midge's wrist. They glowered at each other over his clenched fist. He pushed against her contemptuously, his eyes widening as he felt her strength match his.

Ace spoke through her teeth, 'Sit down and shut up.'

Midge did not relax his grip or his furious stare. Ace sighed. It was High Noon with arm-wrestling every time with this one she thought. She didn't have time to play cowboys and indians. 'Look Midge . . .'

'Listen!' Shreela's urgent whisper made them both turn. They all heard them – slow approaching hoofbeats.

Silently Ace reached for her lighter and flicked the flame, holding it ready by her torch. There was a crash and the sound of struggle in the branches. The trap was sprung. Ace shoved her torch in the flame and tossed the lighter to Shreela. Yelling at the top of her lungs she burst out of the undergrowth. Her face was streaked with dirt like war paint; she waved a burning brand round her head and she was ready for battle.

Paterson lay prone at her feet, holding his arm over his eyes against the glare of her torch. He did not look ready for anything.

Ace skidded to a halt as Shreela arrived at her heels, yelling in her turn. They both stared suspiciously at the cowering Paterson. Ace looked up.

A familiar figure swung upside down from her rope trap, dangling in the thorn trees like an untidy Christmas decoration. One hand still held the battered, white hat firmly on his head. An accusing upside-down stare was levelled at Ace whenever her face swung within reach.

'How many times,' enquired the Doctor severely, 'have I warned you about playing with fire?'

Ace broke into a broad grin. 'What kept you, Professor?'

It was early morning in Perivale. The streets were sunny but still almost empty. An early morning jogger sweated briskly down Ashwood Avenue nodding briefly at a milkman who waved a pint of gold top in reply.

Whistling a garbled selection of Gloria Estefan songs, the milkman walked up to number eighty-three and left the gold top, two pints of low-fat milk and a six-pack of strawberry yoghurt sitting neatly on the step. By then the jogger had panted his way round the corner of the road.

The milkman walked back into the empty street. He chucked a cat under the chin as it basked in the early sun on the garden wall. The large black cat lazily opened its red eyes and watched him walk back to his milkfloat.

★ ★ ★

The Doctor was crawling up the side of a small hill. It had been the work of minutes for Ace to convince the others of his authority: they were at the stage of exhaustion when they would accept any suggestion. Now they wriggled after him, stomachs pressed to the hot and dusty earth.

Only Paterson appeared to be enjoying himself. His wriggle was noisy and energetic; he swung his whole body from side to side and panted strenuously as he levered his way upwards. Sweat flew from his forehead. He was elbowing his way into some dusty dream of obstacle courses, smiling as if he imagined a rope net and a water jump just over the horizon.

'Right, stick together lads, that's the way.'

Ace looked at Shreela. Shreela rolled her eyes meaningfully.

'Stealth, that's what we're after, stealth and surprise. You follow me and I'll get you through this.' Paterson was rapidly approaching the Doctor's heels. 'I'm a hunting animal, got an instinct for it.'

The Doctor spun round abruptly, frowning darkly. 'Shhh!' he hissed in Paterson's face. Paterson subsided in a glowering heap muttering about Swiss army knives.

'Ace?' The Doctor beckoned her to him.

Together they crawled a little distance above the others. The Doctor stared at the sky with a worried expression. Smoke threaded with fire billowed darkly on the horizon.

Ace fidgeted impatiently as she waited for explanations. 'Where are we headed for, Doctor?'

In reply, the Doctor pointed to the smoky horizon. 'It may be nothing, of course, but I think we ought to take a look,' he murmured.

'A look at what?'

The Doctor regarded her seriously for a second. 'At the extent of the deterioration.'

'What?'

'I think the planet's going to explode.'

Ace dropped her head onto her arms and moaned. It was so awful it was almost predictable. Why, she wondered, had she ever hankered for a life of adventure? 'Fine,' she said into her arms. 'Brilliant.'

'Well, it is very old you know,' the Doctor said severely. 'It's bound to be fraying at the edges a bit. Anyway, we'll be much safer over there – no Cheetahs, no Master.'

Ace raised her head. 'Who's this Master?'

'The most evil genius in the universe. One of my oldest and deadliest enemies.'

Ace studied him for a moment. There was only a hint of sarcasm in her next remark. 'Don't you know any nice people, you know, ordinary people? How come it's all power-crazed nutters trying to take over the galaxy?'

'I don't think he's trying to take over the galaxy this time.' The Doctor still peered anxiously at the sky.

'So what's all this in aid of?'

'He hates me.'

Ace sighed. 'They all do,' she muttered.

'And he's the one who's controlling the kitlings, the cats.'

'Why?' Ace asked the question baldly with little hope or expectation of a reply. She got none. The Doctor was deep in thought.

'There's a power-crazed maniac, right,' she said, 'with particularly nasty mental powers. I take it he has got those – they usually do have. Yeah? And this nutter is taking time off conquering galaxies to organize a bunch of pussy-cats to teleport to Earth and send back the good news to the big pussy-cats that there are three-course meals walking round in Perivale, so that they can kidnap my mates, bring them here and chase them round volcanoes.' She paused for breath; she wasn't certain the Doctor was listening. 'And he's doing all this because he hates your guts?' There was still no response. 'And, oh yeah, the planet's going to explode.'

'Yes,' the Doctor said slowly, still scanning the sky.

'Well I'm glad you're sure of something. For a minute there I thought we were really in trouble.'

The Doctor looked at her. 'He must have known you were with me, somehow. But he always has his ways.'

'What?'

'Earth first, that was an obvious choice, but Perivale . . . It can't have been a coincidence; he knew.'

'I'm not getting any of this, Professor.'

'We were hunted, Ace, hunted and trapped. He wanted us here.'

Ace looked at the barren land. Below them, Shreela watched anxiously; Paterson muttered some advice to Midge and Derek. Midge looked away and spat.

'Why did he want us here – apart from wanting to see you get eaten alive?' asked Ace.

The Doctor shook his head. 'I don't know . . . yet. Come on.'

The Doctor wriggled rapidly up to the top of the hill. As Ace followed she saw him peer over the brow to the valley below. He waved his arm. 'Come on everyone,' he called quietly. 'Nothing to worry about.'

As Ace joined him she looked down and drew in her breath sharply. Paterson cursed; Derek gave a low cry.

'Shhh!' The Doctor flapped his hand at them.

A pride of Cheetahs was spread out in the valley below them. The creatures were lying in the middle of a huge spoil-heap of bones, lounging at their ease among the skulls and rib-cages. Some of them chewed on fresher carcasses. The valley was narrow and dark with high sloping walls of black volcanic rock. The golden Cheetahs and the white bones gleamed in the low sunlight.

At the centre of the valley floor was a circular area that had been flattened by the many paws and hooves. Here, two Cheetahs circled each other, snarling and slashing. The others watched the fight as they chewed and scratched. With a snarl one Cheetah leapt at the other.

Derek flinched. The Doctor put a cautioning hand on his arm. 'No sudden movement,' he whispered.

The Master had seen what he was looking for. He smiled, showing the long canines so recently grown in his mouth. With the cat's eyes he shared with the vanished kitling he looked at the Cheetahs. They were growling and panting with hunger. He was just in time.

'The chase,' he whispered.

The Cheetahs turned their heads on one side.

'To run,' whispered the Master.

They growled.

'Hunt.'

They showed their teeth.

'Look.' The Master turned his yellow eyes on them and shared what he saw, what the kitling saw.

They bounded to their feet and sprang for the horses. Horses and riders leaped and vanished.

* * *

In Perivale, two milk bottles smashed on the pavement. The milkman who had dropped them looked up in disbelief and then began to run.

The Master smiled. He called silently, sending the message from his mind to draw another kitling to him. As its dark shape padded across the grass towards him he scooped it up, stroking the thick black fur. Now he could do some hunting of his own.

'Find him,' he whispered in the kitling's ear. 'Hunt him; seek him out; bring me to him.'

The kitling sprang out of his lap. As the Master rose to follow he felt his new, long teeth chewing against his lip. His eyes he knew were still yellow animal's eyes. There was a flash of fire on the horizon. He closed his eyes. 'I must . . . keep . . . control,' he whispered urgently.

The Doctor looked down at the Cheetahs. Their claws and teeth were very much in evidence. He turned to look at the group he had to guide to safety. They all appeared terrified apart from Ace, and even she looked distinctly worried. The Doctor took a deep breath.

'Now,' he said briskly, 'three rules for keeping on the right side of a Cheetah Person. Number one: they won't bother you unless they're hungry. Do these Cheetahs look hungry?' He stared searchingly at each of them in turn.

Below them, one of the Cheetahs yawned. Ace shook her head. Shreela, Midge, Paterson and Derek glanced at each other before reluctantly following suit.

The Doctor beamed. 'Right then.' Very slowly he got to his feet. The others followed.

The Cheetahs watching the fight turned their heads; the sleeping Cheetahs opened their eyes; the fighting

63

Cheetahs stopped clawing at each other. All the Cheetahs looked up at the humans on the slope above them.

'Gently now,' murmured the Doctor and he led them down the slope into the middle of the animals.

Chapter 5

As they stood back to back in a tight group at the centre of the valley, Ace wondered yet again why she had ever thought this lifestyle was appealing. You could get used to Perivale, she reflected as Cheetahs with bared teeth rapidly circled the group. What, after all, was so alarming about the idea of trying to communicate with your own parents, she wondered as a set of claws swiped close to her eyes. Boredom, yes, boredom got to you, but she had never yet heard that it was terminal.

The second thing to remember,' said the Doctor conversationally, 'is that they are essentially a fun-loving species.'

The tatters of Shreela's clothes fluttered in the wind. A Cheetah swiped at the streamers of cloth. Shreela sucked in her breath.

Another Cheetah made a dive on to a trailing shoelace from Derek's shoe. He yelped, jumping back.

'No!' The Doctor gripped his shoulder. 'Don't move!' Pinning Derek with a glare he continued quietly. 'You weren't using that shoe were you?'

Derek looked at the Cheetah staring up at him. He was shaking.

'Take off your shoe, dough brain!' hissed Ace.

Midge bent down, wrenched the trainer from Derek's foot and hurled the shoe away from them. Two Cheetahs fell on it, snarling and clawing.

'You see?' beamed the Doctor. 'Playful.' He led them forward again.

Apart from the Cheetahs that were shredding Derek's trainer, most of the animals had slumped back on the grass, bored with the humans. As they passed the flattened circle of earth the two battling Cheetahs leapt at each other again, claws rending fur.

The group edged nervously past the Cheetahs. Only the Doctor maintained a casual stroll.

The Cheetahs snarled and howled. There was a renewed flash of eruptions on the skyline.

The Doctor paused. 'Is it my imagination,' he murmured, 'or is it growing rather hot?'

Ace glanced anxiously at the lethal struggle that still continued only feet from where they stood. 'Doctor, I think we better keep moving.'

They walked on. Most of the Cheetahs were now behind them. Midge relaxed slightly and quickened his pace. The Doctor held up a warning hand.

'Gently. Keep it casual. We're just taking a little stroll.' He smiled benignly at two recumbent Cheetahs as they circled them. The path ahead was clear. 'You see?' he said jubilantly. 'It's perfectly simple.'

Ace looked back. It seemed to her that a significant number of yellow eyes were still watching them, that pink tongues were running reflectively over teeth.

'The third rule, of course,' continued the Doctor, 'is that once you have passed a Cheetah Person, never, ever, look back.'

Ace snapped her head round. They were approaching the end of the valley. Gradually the Doctor was picking up speed. 'It's really just a matter of keeping your head and allowing for the unexpected,' he tossed over his shoulder.

It was at that moment that the milkman appeared out of the air on the slope above them.

The kitling moved over a landscape of black rocks, leaping agilely from one to the other. Following it, the Master had to pick his way through the boulders. They were making their way down a steep slope. The Master's eyes were on his feet; his thoughts were turned to the quarry he sought – the Doctor. The kitling had picked up a fresh trail and was moving faster. Soon the Master would have his old enemy within his grasp once more.

A low growl jerked the Master from his thoughts. At the foot of the slope, a mounted Cheetah stared up at him. It tore at a piece of flesh it held in one paw. The Creature's eyes fixed on the Master, it paused in mid bite and bared its teeth.

The Master froze. He stared back at the animal; his face was expressionless. He breathed out slowly.

'Get out of my way.' His voice was low and controlled.

The Cheetah tore off another mouthful of flesh and bared its teeth again. It made no other movement.

The Master drew himself up. 'You will get out of my way!' He glared with the full force of his will at the Cheetah.

For a moment the animal stared back at him. Abruptly it spurred its horse forward and clattered away along the gully.

The Master briefly closed his eyes before he began

to follow the kitling again. To anyone watching, he might have appeared to be tired.

The whole scene in the valley full of Cheetahs had remained frozen for a second. The milkman stood where he had staggered out of the air and gazed in amazement at the Doctor, his companions and the animals beyond. They in turn had simply gaped back. The Cheetahs still lay on the grass; the Doctor and the others were checked in their escape up the slope.

A Cheetah on a horse appeared out of the air behind the milkman. It did not pause to study the scene: it saw its prey and charged straight down the hill at him.

The milkman screamed and ran as six mounted Cheetahs appeared behind the first.

'Oh dear,' murmured the Doctor.

'Help me!' screamed the milkman as he fled past them, straight into the waiting claws of the Cheetahs below. They were roused and hungry now.

Derek tried to break to one side as the mounted Cheetahs moved down the slope at them. The Doctor grabbed his arm.

'Don't move!' The commanding power of his voice froze them all.

Ace looked from side to side. Above them the horses had paused. The leading Cheetah bared its teeth at her. She noticed a dark blaze of fur on one side of its face and the cold intelligence of its yellow eyes. She looked down. It was too late to save the milkman, but the Cheetahs which were not feeding had turned from the meal and were staring with renewed interest at the little group of humans. Ace bent to pick up a rock.

'No, Ace!' The Doctor had his eyes fixed on the Cheetahs.

She gaped at him. 'What?'

'There is only one thing more dangerous than being attacked by a Cheetah Person and that's attacking a Cheetah Person. Believe me, you don't know what would happen to you.'

'But Doctor . . .'

'Stay still!'

Ace looked up the slope again. The first Cheetah was starting to descend slowly. Its eyes blazed at her out of the dark fur on its face. She thought it was smiling at her. She looked down. Half crouching, more Cheetahs were creeping up the slope towards them.

Paterson looked wildly from side to side. 'I'm not putting up with this,' he muttered. He was breathing fast; his eyes bulged. Panic trembled in his voice. 'I'm not just going to stand here and get eaten alive!' With a sudden lunge he grabbed the rock from Ace and hurled it at the nearest Cheetah.

'No!' howled the Doctor. He was too late.

Derek broke and ran down the slope, frantically trying to dodge the outstretched claws of the Cheetahs. The mounted Cheetahs spurred their horses to full gallop and thundered down on the group. Midge yelled and grabbed a rock of his own. Below them the other Cheetahs broke into a loping run as Paterson bent to pick up another rock.

'Don't move!' pleaded the Doctor.

Midge's rock caught one of the mounted Cheetahs and knocked it back in the saddle. The other animals snarled as they hurtled forward. The huge horses seemed about to trample the humans down.

Paterson ran first, then Midge. Shreela held her ground for a second before following. Ace saw the powerful legs and shoulders of the nearest horse

69

pistoning down on her – she ran out of pure instinct. Only the Doctor remained motionless as the horses and riders swept past him. All his companions were running for their lives; each was pursued by a pack of Cheetahs.

On high ground above the valley, a kitling looked down. It saw a mêlée of bodies: Cheetahs and humans tumbled and ran in all directions. Only one figure stood motionless, both hands clasping a battered hat to his head as if he feared for its safety above all else.

With footsteps as soft as the kitling's own, the Master came to stand beside it. He too looked down. He drew in his breath sharply. A smile bared the thin canines in his mouth: his quarry was sighted.

There was a menacing rumble from the other side of the horizon.

Derek was lying on the ground between two Cheetahs. A third circled him on its horse. They were playing with him, rolling him from one to the other. Each blow of their paws gashed him with razor sharp claws. Derek tried to curl up to protect his head. His face was bleeding.

A stone slammed into one of the Cheetahs, hitting it on the flank. It turned, snarling. Ace was already bending down for another handful of stones. She straightened up, breathing fast, and looked from one to the other of the Cheetahs.

'Come on then,' she said, her own teeth bared.

All three animals turned on her. Ace hurled the first rock high. It hit the Cheetah on the horse below the dark blaze of fur on the creature's face. The Cheetah fell forward over the horse's neck. One of the other Cheetahs turned, distracted; the other kept coming.

Ace saw Derek stumble to his feet and make his escape.

She hurled her next rock.

The Doctor stood still as Shreela panted past him, eyes wide, hair flying behind her. The Cheetah pursuing her raked its claws into her hair. Shreela screamed. Deftly the Doctor stuck his umbrella out, tangling the animal's legs. The Cheetah fell snarling as the Doctor politely raised his hat. The creature scrambled up and bounded after Shreela but she had vanished over the edge of the valley.

The Doctor looked round wildly. Where was Ace? More Cheetahs approached. He forced himself to remain motionless.

Midge and Paterson were running. Several Cheetahs were hot on their heels, but without the spur of real hunger the animals were content to move at a loping trot that allowed them to jab their claws into the men's backs.

The valley forked. Paterson dived up one gully, Midge up another.

Midge glanced over his shoulder and saw with a sob of fear that all the Cheetahs were following him.

Activity in the valley gradually ceased. All the humans had been pursued, and the hunters and hunted were out of sight. Only the Doctor stood exactly as he had been. A few of the animals circled him, sniffing, but gradually they turned away.

Cheetahs yawned and flopped gracefully back on to the warm grass to doze. Those that had been hungry were still chewing and squabbling over what was left of the milkman; the rest were in no real mood for a hunt. One by one they all relaxed. The strange, almost formal ritual of the fight began again on the flattened

71

arena of earth at the centre of the valley. Soon none of the animals were even looking at the Doctor.

The Doctor made one last anxious survey of the valley. He had not even seen in which direction Ace had fled in the general mayhem. Sighing, he straightened his hat on his head and walked slowly and carefully out of the valley towards the volcanoes. He did not see the kitling padding along his trail or the dark shadow of the Master behind it.

Ace had begun to identify a pattern in the actions of the animal that pursued her. It would match her pace, accelerate occasionally to dart in front of her and lash out with teeth and claws to startle her on to a new path.

It didn't matter how fast – or how slow – her stumbling progress was. She was being chivvied and harried over the hot rocks. Only when she was too exhausted for the game to continue would the Cheetah unleash its real strength and finish her off.

With her breath wheezing in her throat, Ace knew she had to find some escape soon. Her feet stumbled; the Cheetah darted in front of her again and jabbed its claws into her, snapping at her face. Ace swerved again. She didn't see the cliff. Her scream was carried over the edge as she tumbled and somersaulted down the dusty slope below.

The Cheetah hesitated at the top of the cliff and peered after her. Ace had vanished into the boulders at the base of the cliffs. The dust of her headlong fall was beginning to settle, but the Cheetah could see no movement. Cautiously, it loped down the steep slope after her.

On the other side of the boulders, a small lake glinted in the dim sunlight. Its edges lapped against the shore, tiny waves caused by the hot wind that blew round the rocks. Nothing else moved.

The Cheetah slowly turned its head, its wide, yellow eyes scanning every inch of the rocks. There was a flicker among the boulders; the creature's head snapped round, ears pointing and alert. A lizard scuttled out of sight. The Cheetah relaxed again. It sniffed the air. There was a strong trace of the young woman's smell but it was fading fast. It blinked as it looked around again. The heat reflected off the boulders, blasting its fur with warmth. The Cheetah yawned. The day was too hot for hunting and its stomach was full. Slowly it turned away and vanished into the rocks.

In an eruption of spray, Ace burst up from the water, coughing and wheezing. She dragged herself on to the warm shore and lay there, all her remaining strength concentrated on dragging as much air as she could into her lungs.

Midge didn't know it but only one Cheetah still pursued him, walking its horse casually up the valley after him. The others had long since flopped down to squabble and doze in the dust. Midge didn't know this because he was no longer aware of anything except the continuous thunder of his blood in his ears and the agonizing effort of keeping his legs moving in a stumbling run.

At last he collapsed, his legs crumpled under him and he lay breathing dust in laboured, sobbing breaths. There was no sound but that for a moment – then he heard the horse's hoofs. He pulled his face out of the ground and looked around.

The Cheetah sat motionless on its horse. It just watched him with its yellow eyes, its fur ruffling in the wind. Midge stumbled to his feet. At once the Cheetah kicked its horse forward. Sobbing, Midge turned and tried to run again.

The valley in which the Doctor found himself was dark: the walls were too high for the sun to rise above them but it was still hot. A pulse of red throbbed through clouds of smoke in the sky above him like a great heart.

The Doctor smelled sulphur. Pools beside his path steamed and bubbled – he was very close to the volcanoes. Suddenly he stopped. Ahead of him were rocks that were not just tumbled haphazardly by landslides. Shaped stones lay in heaps, the remains of high walls. He saw broken arches and the remains of a dome that must have made a massive vault over the valley. It was the ruins of a huge building such as a palace or a cathedral. The statues and decorative stonework that might have suggested its purpose were weathered to vague blurs.

The Doctor slowly walked up to it. Each block of stone was the size of a small cottage but its edges had been skilfully and precisely shaped to a perfect rectangle.

He was pondering the skill of the vanished architects when a dark shape leapt yowling at his face. The Doctor yelled and jumped back. The kitling crouched among the ruins and stared up at him. All the fur on its back stood upright and prickling.

The Doctor heard a low chuckle behind him.

'Good hunting, Doctor.'

The Doctor turned and faced his enemy again. The Master stood motionless in the shadow of the ruins. He was waiting. In spite of himself, the Doctor shivered.

The Master: he had never had a more dangerous adversary, nor one with whom he shared so much history. The Master was also a Time Lord. They had been at school together, although school was probably an inappropriate description of that ancient and awful house of learning. They had both rebelled against the ponderous, measured ordering of the universe required by the Council of the Time Lords and since then, in their separate wanderings across time and space, their paths had crossed many, many times.

Perhaps they had once had similar dreams of freedom and adventure. In the many centuries since then, the Doctor had become the wanderer he now was – always an outsider, always unpredictable, an inexplicable question mark in the pattern of the universe where everything was, finally, explicable by those that had the power. Whatever the Doctor was, his effect was benign if chaotic. The Master was a thing of malice.

Looking now into the familiar dark eyes, the Doctor wondered yet again what had so embittered the other Time Lord to make him wish harm to every living creature in existence.

The Master had caused great harm: the beings he had killed or enslaved, the planets and galaxies he had held in his power were countless. All that appeared to give him pleasure was random cruelty and the acquisition of power, but even that enjoyment was short-lived because he despised whatever he controlled. Only obsession drove him now, the desire to be revenged on those who had forced him into exile and his desperate need to destroy one being, the Doctor.

Perhaps, the Doctor reflected, if the Master had defeated him just once – even long ago when they had been learning together – if the other Time Lord could remember even one occasion when he had shone at the Doctor's expense and when the final victory had been his, perhaps their whole history might have been different.

The Doctor remembered how the other had longed to excel, to prove himself the greatest and be master of them all. But the Doctor had always been one degree better, one step ahead; worse, the Doctor did not care whether he won.

In all their subsequent encounters, the Master had sought to destroy the Doctor while the Doctor tried only to prevent the Master from harming others. The Master pursued the Doctor across the universe. The Doctor did not care whether he ever saw the Master again. It was this, he realized, that was unforgivable.

In the early days he had carried off the prizes and the praise that the Master so desperately wanted from their teachers, but the Doctor had not valued the prizes and he was indifferent to the praise. He had robbed the Master of his position at the top and he had humiliated him by his casual attitude to what was the other Time Lord's whole reason for being.

Now the Master pursued him with hatred, continually forcing him into confrontations, power struggles and duels to the death. The Master had spent hundreds of years plotting the Doctor's destruction, but the Doctor gave no indication that he ever thought of his enemy unless he had to. What his attitude implied was that he had more important things to think about, and that was unforgivable.

The Doctor sighed. It was probably unfortunate that he had not considered all of this several millennia earlier when he could simply have let the Master beat him at chess.

He waited for the other to speak again. The Master

simply stood for a long moment, petting the heavy kitling that had climbed into his arms. He watched the other Time Lord. The Doctor could not read his expression but he could swear that the Master was gloating.

Ace had finally started to breathe normally. She lay still at the edge of the water, her head pillowed on her arms. As her breathing slowed and quietened she felt exhaustion creeping along every bone and muscle. The sun steamed the moisture out of her clothes. She couldn't move; she just lay there blinking sleepily at the pattern of light on the water.

The sun glinted off each wavelet in a pattern that blurred to a sparkling dazzle as Ace's eyes focused and defocused. She did not know how long she had lain there before she noticed the colour of the light had changed. A warm, pink light made a path across the water. Slowly, Ace raised her head and looked up.

The planet's moon was rising, a soft globe of peach-coloured light. Ace gazed up for a long moment. In her exhaustion the moon seemed the most peaceful, soothing thing she had seen for as long as she could remember.

She heard hoofs approaching and staggered to her feet. She darted into the shelter of nearby boulders and crouched there, peering out.

On the other side of the lake a Cheetah Person on a horse was approaching. It seemed as if it was barely conscious; the creature slumped forward in the saddle. The horse headed to the water's edge to drink, carrying its rider with it. As the horse's head dropped to the water, the Cheetah roused slightly. It looked round blearily before dismounting – it almost fell in the attempt. It slid on to all fours and crawled to the water to drink in its turn. Its head bent, it lapped a little water. Slowly its head came up again. It seemed to be staring straight across the lake at Ace.

Ace caught her breath and tried to flatten herself further into the boulders. The Cheetah had a dark blaze of fur on its face. It was the animal that had eaten Stuart, the Cheetah that had led the attack on the milkman. It was the same creature that Ace had struck with her second rock; she could see the wound on its head.

The Cheetah's gaze shifted. Ace realized it was looking past her into the sky. She turned.

Another tranquil moon was rising in the sky behind her, spreading more warm light over the water. As Ace gazed at it she heard an unearthly yowl. Her head snapped round again.

The Cheetah was baying at the moon. Its head was thrown back and its furry throat throbbed with the cry. Ace watched wide-eyed. The animal threw back its head to howl again but the sound changed to a choking cough. Panting, it lowered its head and tried to lap again at the lake. There was blood in the water where its mouth had been. Its eyes were half-closed; it breathed in quick shallow breaths, its sides heaving. For a third time it lowered its head. This time it slipped under the water up to its shoulders. It didn't move again.

Ace peered further out of her hiding place. The Cheetah still didn't move. Slowly Ace stood up. She was poised to run.

A few bubbles of air broke the surface beside the animal's head. Ace began slowly to walk towards the creature but quickly broke into a run. She hestated once she reached the motionless Cheetah.

Its horse cropped grass peacefully beside them,

78

undisturbed. The Cheetah lay submerged, there were no air-bubbles now. Bending abruptly Ace heaved at the body and pulled it clear of the water. She rolled it onto its back.

The Cheetah lay with its eyes closed; it did not appear to be breathing. Ace studied it. It had been lighter than she expected and its fur was soft to the touch. Looking at it now she saw how human its shape was. It was a female, like a woman covered in short-haired fur. The ears were flat to its skull, its terrifying yellow eyes hidden. It seemed smaller too, hardly any taller than Ace.

Curiously Ace leaned over to touch it again. Like a cat, its fur ran in one direction. She stroked it down, feeling its smooth softness under her hand.

The Cheetah's eyes opened and it stared up at her.

Midge was crawling along the ground. The heat of the sun hammered in his head like the pounding of his heart. His knees and the palms of his hands had been torn by the rocks. He no longer knew why he was moving. He could hear the hoofbeats, slow now behind him and the sound still drove him forward.

At last he raised his head. He was back in the valley he had first run from. Blinking dazedly he recognized the slope the milkman had run down, the heaps of bones and the flattened circle of earth where the two Cheetah People had engaged in their ritual fight. Although the valley was now deserted, he knew it was the same place. His desperate flight had simply taken him in a circle. With a groan Midge collapsed to the ground. He had no strength to go further.

He heard the hoofbeats approach to within feet of him and then stop. He opened his eyes. The Cheetah had dismounted, its smooth furry feet were close by his face, the long claws flexing. Midge closed his eyes and waited for the end. There was a pause, then Midge felt a draught and a spray of dust as the animal ran past him. He heard a low warning growl and dragged his head out of the dust.

Another Cheetah was approaching from the other end of the valley. It loped forward in a crouch, its claws extended and teeth bared. The Cheetah that had been pursuing Midge ran to meet it. They circled each other round the flattened area of earth. Midge could now see that the ground around it was marked with blood.

As he watched, the two animals leapt at each other, spitting and clawing as they wrestled each other. Midge lay and watched, waiting for the fight to finish and the victor to come and kill him.

There was a huge eruption behind the hills. Red, liquid rock spouted into the air. The Doctor and the Master looked up.

'They're fighting again,' said the Master, 'fighting in the Dead Valley.'

The Doctor watched the explosions. 'It's breaking up. The planet's breaking up.'

The Master started to walk slowly towards him. 'This planet is alive,'he said. 'The animals are part of the planet. When they fight each other in that place, the Dead Valley, they trigger explosions – they create the planet's destruction.'

The Doctor nodded. 'How long before the planet blows up?'

'Not long. The animals have been fighting for generations.'

The Master was close to him now. The Doctor waited but he said nothing else. He fidgeted impatiently before bursting out, 'Why did you bring me here?'

The Master stared at him for a second. There was something in his expression that the Doctor did not understand. But as the other continued to glare at him, he began to see what there was behind the tight control of his features. It was composed of rage and bitterness, and the Master was not gloating at all.

A tight smile broke on the other Time Lord's face. His voice, like his expression, was rigidly controlled as he said what must have stuck in his throat. 'I need you, Doctor. I need your help.'

The Doctor let the words echo round the rocks. They both knew the enormity of that request. He put his head on one side and studied the Master curiously. 'Why,' he said at last, 'should I help you?'

The Master did not answer at once, he was looking round at the ruins that surrounded them. 'This used to be a huge civilization,' he remarked conversationally. 'Their cities covered the whole planet. Now there's nothing – even the ruins are nearly all dust. They had an empire and fleets of starships; they'd developed their mental powers to a remarkable degree. The power of their minds for telepathy and control almost approached my own.' His voice trailed off.

'What happened to them?' the Doctor asked bluntly. The Master made no reply. He simply stared at the ancient stones.

The Doctor sighed. 'You need my help. I take it you are offering something in return? Perhaps you could begin by telling me how my companions and I can escape from here.'

The Master turned to look at him, a bleak look. 'My dear Doctor,' he said wearily, 'you seem to have become quite annoyingly obtuse.'

81

The Doctor stared at him then realization dawned. 'You're trapped!'

'Just so,' the Master said drily. 'The doors into this world are one-way only.'

The Doctor stared at the kitling that the Master held. Suddenly he understood everything. He understood what he had felt from the kitlings, what he had felt ever since he arrived. It was the planet. The Master was right, the planet was alive: its rocks, its water and its trees all had an extra dimension. It was as if the fierce animals of the planet breathed the substance of the place and their blood pulsed with its rivers of lava. As they fought, the planet erupted; as they slept or watched its moons, the whole world grew stiller. Each was part of the other. It was the wild energy of the planet that gave the animals their savagery and the power to leap from world to world; it was the tug of the planet that brought them home again with whatever they had seized. But only the animals could leave and only the animals could return. The power came from the planet and what was not part of the planet had no power here at all.

'So we're both trapped,' the Doctor said slowly.

'I thought that in the circumstances two heads might be better than one, so I brought you here. You are ridiculously easy to track down, Doctor.'

'How did you get here?'

The Master sighed. 'It was a particularly bloody little war I'd arranged in the Antari system. It was entertaining at first but soon degenerated into nothing more refined than pure butchery. I needed a rapid exit; I followed the nearest kitling.' He shrugged.

The Doctor looked into the kitling's red eyes. Again he felt the persistent pulse of its communication; the voice of the whole wild planet clamoured to enter his mind.

'You talk to them,' he said.

'You of all people have reason to know my mental powers, Doctor.'

The Doctor shook his head. 'I won't let them in,' he said.

'Perhaps you are wise.'

The Doctor looked up sharply. The Master's expression was unreadable. 'So, Doctor, we had better hurry and find our escape while enough of your little friends remain to divert the Cheetah People.'

The Doctor scowled. 'If you think you can threaten me into . . .'

'Listen, you fool!' interrupted the Master, 'You are wasting time and time is something we have in short supply!'

His urgency silenced the Doctor. Controlling himself, the Master continued more calmly. 'This planet has an effect on everything that comes here Doctor, an effect no one can escape, not even a Time Lord. It happened to the people who built their cities here. They developed a mind link with the kitlings as I have; they thought they could live in the wilderness and control it, but the wilderness broke in on them.' The Master closed his eyes and turned away. 'The planet is alive, Doctor. You have to save me to save yourself.'

'Save myself from what?' the Doctor said sharply. 'Your pets?'

The Master gave a bitter laugh. As he turned back, the Doctor saw that his eyes had become the yellow eyes of a cat. He was breathing fast.

'I don't control the Cheetahs, Doctor. You might say that they control me.' As he bared his teeth in a mirthless grin, the Doctor saw the long canines in his jaw for the first time.

'I can use the kitlings,' he continued. He was panting now, yellow eyes staring. 'I can provide distractions. My will is strong enough for that, but it gets weaker every hour. Soon I will not be able to control them. Soon I will just run and forget. You have no idea of the humiliation that will overtake us, Doctor, the indignity. There is no escape.'

He stepped forward; the Doctor stepped back.

'Even the will of a Time Lord cannot hold out against this place. We have to leave now or we will leave too late!'

His yellow eyes were close to the Doctor's own. Pointed teeth gleamed in his mouth. The Doctor took another step back. 'But no one can leave,' he faltered, 'except one of the animals.'

The Master's lips drew back further from his teeth. 'Yes,' he hissed, 'that is what anyone who survives here becomes – what the builders of this city became; what we will all become: one of the animals.'

As the Doctor stared at him in horror, the Master's gaze slid past him. He stared up at the sky for a moment. Above them the soft, peachy moons hung above the silhouettes of the ruined walls. As if compelled the Master threw back his head and howled a long, throbbing, inhuman cry.

The Doctor stepped back again. The Master no longer even seemed to be aware that he was there. As the Doctor turned and fled from the valley, he heard the Master howl again. The call was answered by other animals in the rocks.

Ace had moved back from the Cheetah. She watched warily as it coughed up water and blood. It curled up protectively, making little growling moans and holding itself. Finally, the coughing stopped. It looked up at Ace, panting, and reached out a paw to her. Ace flinched but held herself still as the animal's movement slowed. The Cheetah pulled gently at one of her badges. 'Bright.'

Ace jumped in shock. It was no more than a purring whisper but the animal had spoken.

'Shining,' it purred. It looked up at Ace.

Ace stared back into the wide yellow eyes and held her breath. Something in the animal's eyes seemed to speak to her, a strange wild feeling that she half recognized. This was no mere animal.

As if in confirmation the Cheetah nodded her head. 'Karra,' she whispered, 'I am Karra.' Her mouth opened, baring her teeth in a cat-like grin. She pulled at the badge again. 'Nice,' she purred. Her eyes closed.

Ace bent over her quickly, trying to determine whether she was still breathing. The yellow eyes opened again, alarmingly close to her own. 'Moon water,' hissed Karra. Ace frowned. 'Moon water,' she said again, her eyes sliding past Ace to look at the lake.

Ace turned. The two moons were close together in the sky, making a track of flesh-coloured light across the water towards them.

'It will make me well,' breathed Karra in her low, throaty purr, 'very fast.'

Hesitantly, Ace got up and moved towards the water's edge. She looked back at Karra. The Cheetah was watching her, panting, the tip of her tongue just visible through her lethal teeth. Ace bent and scooped up the water. It glowed in her cupped hands as if lit from within. Ace gasped in wonder and let it run

85

flickering back into the water. She scooped up another shining handful and carried it back to Karra.

The Cheetah lapped from Ace's palm, her tongue rough and hot against the girl's skin, then she let her head drop forward on to her paws.

'Better soon,' she growled sleepily. Her breathing grew even.

Ace drew herself close and settled down to watch Karra sleep. She had no memory now of being afraid.

Midge stared at the two Cheetahs as he had stared for long moments as they snarled and clawed and tore blood from each other. Now they lay still. Midge moved at last. He heaved himself out the dust and blinked.

Both Cheetahs were sprawled, one half collapsed across the other, in the centre of the arena of trampled earth. The wind blew torn clumps of their fur down the dusty valley. They were motionless; they seemed to be dead. As this realization slowly dawned on Midge, he pulled himself to his feet.

He began to stagger towards the fallen animals. There was no sound but his dragging footsteps and the wind whining down the valley. He looked down at the Cheetahs. They lay sprawled in their own blood. Midge bent closer.

One of them opened its yellow eyes and stared up at him.

Midge felt a shock of recognition, the sense of something powerful and dangerous reaching out to him. He stepped back. Something clattered under his feet. Midge turned.

He had disturbed the skull of some huge carnivore. One of its teeth had fallen from its jaw. Midge bent and picked it up. The white and gleaming tooth was heavy in his hands and its point was razor sharp. Midge looked at it for a second before turning slowly towards the dying animal. He stared again into its eyes and felt the wildness growing in him. He moved closer and raised the great tooth.

With a scream, Midge plunged the weapon with all his strength into the animal's heart. It gave a yowling cry and lay still.

Midge looked down at its body. Gradually he felt the terror and exhaustion ebbing from him. He felt invincible.

Shreela crouched in the undergrowth near the valley with Paterson and Derek. Since they had found each other, they had remained in hiding.

Shreela looked miserably at the other two. If she was to die she could have wished for better company. Derek was muttering something, the same words repeated over and over. Paterson was simply staring into space: he seemed to be in shock. Strange howls came from the barren hills around them. Shreela looked at the two moons that had risen in the sky and shivered. She caught Paterson's eye. He gave a ghastly grin and tried to straighten himself up.

'Don't you worry,' he said hoarsely. 'I'll sort all this out.'

Shreela nodded and smiled weakly. There seemed little point in reminding him of the hopelessness of their situation.

There was a rumble from the volcanoes. A renewed chorus of howls came from the rocks close by. Shreela looked round.

Midge was walking towards them. His arms were bloody to the elbow and he carried a great tooth in his hands.

★ ★ ★

Ace was still watching the sleeping Cheetah, Karra. The creature's breathing was peaceful now; her sides rose and fell regularly; her whiskers twitched with her breaths. Curiously, Ace reached out to touch them.

'Ace.'

The familiar voice made her spin round grinning. The Doctor stood on the slope above her, watching her seriously.

'I knew you'd get away,' Ace beamed. She noticed his expression. 'What is it?'

The Doctor did not answer. He walked closer and looked down at Karra. Ace turned back to the sleeping animal.

'Should we leave her, Doctor?' her voice was soft.

'If we leave it, it might die.'

Ace looked up at him. 'Should I let her die?'

The Doctor did not answer at once, but when he did his voice was grave. 'Cheetah People are extremely dangerous creatures. This is a very dangerous place, very ancient and very dangerous.' The Doctor looked round the landscape, staring towards the volcanoes. 'It's too old,' he muttered. 'A planet that's lived beyond its own time. It was here at the beginning of everything.'

Ace was still looking at the Cheetah. 'I think it's the one that chased me – the one that killed that boy.' She looked up. The Doctor was watching her intently. 'Her name's Karra,' she said.

The Doctor nodded. 'She could be very useful to us,' he said softly.

'You mean she could help us get home?' Ace asked eagerly.

The Doctor hesitated. 'What we need,' he said slowly, 'Is an animal whose home is earth.'

Ace tried to make sense of that and failed. The

Doctor was still watching her intently with something that looked like fear. She shrugged. 'Better keep her alive then, eh?' She stood up to go and fetch more moon water.

'Ace.'

She turned. The Doctor was frightened, she thought, but why?

'It could be very dangerous for you.'

Ace grinned. 'Don't worry, Professor, I'm no one's bowl of cat food.' She walked down to the lake.

Watching from the boulders behind them, the Master gave a slow smile of satisfaction. The Doctor's words rang again in his head: an animal whose home is Earth. The Master understood how he could escape.

Paterson felt he had a team now. They depended on him and were bound to look to him for leadership, he thought.

He walked up and down under the trees making a shaky attempt at his old, blustering manner. Derek, Shreela and Midge watched him. He avoided catching Midge's eye: whatever the boy had been through it seemed to have left him in a very unstable frame of mind.

'Right!' Paterson clapped his hands briskly. 'You just follow the sarge and I'll get us all out of here. There's nothing I don't know about survival: it's kill or be killed, right? Kill or be killed.'

Midge watched him intently, his bloody arms resting on his knees. 'Kill or be killed,' he repeated softly.

Paterson glanced at him nervously. Perhaps the lad just needed someone to give him a lead, he thought. It would give him a sense of security.

'That's right lad,' he said heartily. 'You're going to

89

come through – we're going to come through. Just follow the sarge. Are you with me?'

'Yes,' said Midge. Derek and Shreela simply looked bemused.

'Are you all with me!' demanded Paterson with growing confidence.

'Yeah!' shouted Midge.

Paterson leaned over the three of them and lowered his voice, jabbing his finger at them emphatically. 'Well, you better get with me because if we're going to survive we can't carry shirkers and we can't carry dead wood.'

'No dead wood,' Midge repeated softly. He turned and stared at the bewildered Derek with a horrible intensity.

Ace bent for another handful of water. She looked up at the two moons, marvelling again at their gentle light. She let her eyes wander over the rest of the landscape. She was suddenly aware of the feel of the wind against her skin. The shadows on the rocks showed her the shape of the land; she felt as if she could reach out and stroke it. She smelt water, hot rocks and a distant, sharp, spicy smell she thought must be the thorn trees. She smelt a warm animal scent that seemed to come from her own hands where she had touched Karra's fur. All of it was somehow familiar.

'Where are the others?' she said slowly.

'I don't know,' replied the Doctor. 'We have to find them soon.'

Ace nodded, but she could feel no urgency. 'It's weird, Doctor,' she said still looking at the landscape, 'I think I like this place. I like it – I feel as if I belong here somehow.'

'Connected,' the Doctor said quietly behind her.

Ace nodded without turning. 'I'm not scared. It feels exciting.'

'What do you feel?' the Doctor said sharply.

Ace considered. 'Like I could run for miles.' She sniffed the air. 'I can smell things as clear as seeing pictures.'

'Anything else?'

'Well.' Ace thought about it, then laughed. 'I'm starving, Professor.'

She turned and grinned at him. He did not smile back.

Somewhere beyond the boulders on the other side of the lake someone began to scream. It sounded like Shreela. Ace and the Doctor looked at each other, turned and ran in the direction of the noise.

The sound came from a clearing in the thorn trees ahead of them. As they burst out of the undergrowth they saw Paterson circling helplessly as Midge and Derek rolled over and over on the ground. Shreela was trying to drag them apart.

'Stop it, Midge!' she screamed. 'Stop it!'

Midge's tooth-knife was inches from Derek's throat.

'Midge!' The Doctor's voice was a command.

Midge turned. The Doctor and Ace looked at the blood on his arms. There was something hanging round his neck – a necklace of Cheetah claws and skin.

'He's going to get us all killed,' Midge jerked his knife at Derek, 'unless someone sorts him out.'

'Sorts him out?' The Doctor's voice was grave.

Midge hefted his knife and grinned. 'Yeah.'

'Where did you get the claws, Midge?' The Doctor took a step towards him.

Midge hefted his knife again warningly. 'I killed it,' he whispered. He looked round at them all and then started to laugh. He banged his chest triumphantly. 'I killed it!'

Paterson cleared his throat nervously and took a step forward.

'Now then, lad, why don't you just, eh, just put the knife down now.'

Midge stared up at him for one contemptuous moment and suddenly leapt up at the sergeant, pointing the tooth at Paterson's face. Paterson stepped back hastily. Midge grinned, turned and stalked out of the clearing.

'Midge!' shouted the Doctor.

Midge froze but did not turn.

'It's not too late,' said the Doctor, 'to come home.'

Midge turned and stared back at the Doctor. He stared with yellow cat's eyes. As everyone stepped back in shock at this transformation, Midge bared his sharp new canines in a snarl and loped out of sight.

Shreela looked at the Doctor with horror, but with the beginnings of hope. 'Home?' she whispered.

He nodded grimly. 'I hope so. There's a chance for some of us.' He looked in the direction Midge had vanished. 'Come on, we have to follow him.'

The kitlings were already following him. They swarmed round every tree and rock, lurking like shadows and waiting for the prey they had been alerted to. As Midge loped past, one of them gave a warning growl. Its red eyes shared their vision.

In a nearby valley, the Master gave a smile of triumph as he saw Midge loping past in his mind's eye, yellow eyes blazing, teeth bared. The Master stood up. He had been cutting strips of leather from a carcass; he had them in his hands now, knotted into a long, whip-like lasso. He raised it and snapped it. He began to run in the direction the kitlings had shown him.

Midge sped across flat ground. He was aware of a new strength in his limbs, the ground rushed by under his feet. The motion felt good. He could smell blood from the dried stains on his own arms. He sniffed it eagerly, the scent seemed to give even greater strength to his limbs. He was not consciously thinking of anything but the sensation of running and his desire to find more blood. He was unaware of the changes that were happening to him. It felt right that he should see, hear and smell as he did, with new strengthened senses. It felt like this was what he wanted to be. Midge put on a new burst of speed and growled happily.

The Master stepped out from a rock in front of him, the lasso held loosely in his hands.

Midge stopped and snarled.

The Doctor led them at a brisk trot along Midge's trail. His eyes were bent on footprints or other signs of Midge's passing while his brain worked furiously. Once the power of the planet awoke in you, what then? You would share in its strength, its wildness and its savagery, but would you also remember other rocks, other winds, the stone and water of the place that had once made you? Would you be tugged by your own world as the Cheetah planet tugged its creatures home?

'Quickly!' The Doctor broke into a run and led them up another valley. 'This way.'

* * *

Midge struggled in the dirt and clawed at the noose around his neck. The Master jerked at the lasso, pulling Midge towards him. He pulled the boy up until their faces were inches from each other. Cat's eyes stared into cat's eyes.

'Go hunting,' whispered the Master.

Midge's face went slack and blank.

The Master smiled. 'Go home.'

Midge got up. The Master held him by the noose like a dog on a lead. Midge sniffed at the air as if searching for something.

The Doctor and the others ran out of cover. The others halted and stared as the Doctor darted forward. 'Midge!'

Midge did not even turn his head. The Master laughed. He was gloating now, smiling triumphantly at the Doctor as he held Midge's lead. 'You see, Doctor, you did help me. You kept these others alive just long enough to serve my purposes.

The Doctor ran closer and reached out to the transformed creature that had been Midge. 'Midge wait!'

Midge turned his yellow eyes slowly towards the Doctor and stared at him coldly.

The Master indicated Ace and the others watching horrified from some distance away. 'Don't worry, Doctor, one of them will become a Cheetah animal before you; you can escape in your turn or are you too squeamish? Only the animals of this place can leave, Doctor, because then they carry it with them.'

The Doctor was not listening. He moved to stand in front of Midge. 'Midge, listen to me!'

Midge stared at him blankly for a second before baring his teeth.

The Master smiled. 'He doesn't remember his

name.' He bent forward and whispered in Midge's ear. 'Go home.'

Midge's head came up, his eyes widened and he leapt into the air. He and the Master vanished.

Slowly, the others came to stand round the Doctor. They stared at the place where Midge used to be.

'So there is a way out,' said Shreela in wonder.

The Doctor sighed. 'A way out? Yes. We wait until some of us turn wild and then we try to use them before they escape or kill the rest of us.' He stared miserably at the ground as the others looked at each other nervously.

Paterson cleared his throat. 'Well, no telling who'll be first, eh? Just need to, eh, keep a grip and, eh – what are you looking at!' He shot this out at Derek who was gaping at him slack mouthed.

Derek began to giggle and shake, his eyes wide and frightened.

Paterson backed away from him. 'He's gone hasn't he?' he squeaked, pointing a trembling finger at Derek. 'He's gone! Look, keep away from me, lad!' He turned to the others. 'We better finish him off now or . . .'

Look!' Shreela's shout interrupted him. She pointed to the other end of the valley.

A Cheetah Person sat on its horse, straight-backed and motionless. It had a dark blaze of fur on its face and its eyes were fixed on Ace.

'Oh yeah! She's better!' Ace ran a few eager steps towards the Cheetah. 'Doctor, look!' She turned back to grin at him.

The Doctor saw in horror that her eyes were the cold, wild, yellow of the Cheetah People's.

Chapter 6

The street outside the block of flats was empty. It was the time of day when kids were at school, adults were at work and those without work had just tuned in to the first of the day's Australian soap operas. There was no one to see Midge leap out of the air, pulling the Master after him by the lead round his neck.

Midge stood with his shoulders hunched, his face slack. His eyes were still the eyes of a Cheetah Person but there was no savagery, no purpose of any kind left in him now. He looked around in bewilderment. The Master did the same with an expression of deep distaste.

'Where is this?' asked the Master.

Midge shook his head as if to clear it. 'Home,' he said dazedly. He turned away, pulling his lead out of the Master's hand. He started to wander towards the entrance to the flats.

The Master quickly looked round to see if they were observed and then followed.

Ace was walking slowly towards Karra, who dismounted and came to meet her. The others all began to retreat; only the Doctor stood his ground.

Ace looked into Karra's hypnotic eyes. She could see her own reflection in their yellow mirror, a woman with cat's eyes of her own.

'Come hunting, sister,' purred Karra.

Ace hesitated. Her whole instinct was to leap forward and join the Cheetah woman but something still held her back.

'Ace, wait!' The Doctor's voice tugged at her memory. She frowned, trying to remember. It was dangerous for her to join this strange woman, but why?

'Come hunting,' Karra purred again.

Ace looked into her golden eyes and forgot she had anything to worry about. She forgot everything except what it would be like to stretch every muscle running flat out across the plain. She smiled. She took a step forward.

'No, Ace!'

She hardly heard the Doctor's call. She saw Karra's teeth bared in a grin; she saw Karra's muscles rippling under her fur as she turned and leapt forward. Ace followed, feeling her legs swallowing the ground beneath her as she sped for the horizon behind the Cheetah woman, laughing from sheer pleasure.

'Ace!' Shreela called after her, running forward to join the Doctor. Together they watched as Ace and Karra receded. Only the sound of Ace's laughter drifted back to them.

Shreela looked fearfully at the Doctor. 'It's happened hasn't it? It's happened to her. She's changing.'

The Doctor stared at Ace, flying away from him across the plain. It didn't seem possible that anything human could move so fast. 'Yes,' he said quietly, 'she's changed.'

'Who's next, eh? Who's next?' Paterson began to pace nervously. 'If I had a gun . . .'

'We'd be in even more trouble than we already are.' The Doctor cut him off abruptly. 'Right, stay here. I'll go and find Ace.'

'Now just a minute . . .' Paterson began to bluster.

The Doctor turned a radiantly insincere smile on him. 'I can leave you in charge, can't I sergeant?'

Paterson frowned. 'Well, if you put it like that.'

The Doctor turned to leave, winking broadly at Shreela. She caught anxiously at his arm. 'But what if more Cheetahs come?'

The Doctor considered. 'Sit very still and try not to look like hamburger,' he advised. He looked at three of them all watching him with glum and nervous apprehension. 'Cheer up,' he said, 'it could be worse.' He glanced at the sky. 'It could be raining.'

He gave a cheery wave and began to jog after Ace.

Ace laughed as she ran. She laughed from the sheer pleasure of her movement. The wind rushed past her face and tugged her hair out behind her. The ground sped away under her feet and she never stumbled. They could, she thought, keep running for ever. After that she thought of nothing except the smell of the wind.

The Doctor paused, breathless, in his pursuit. There was no way he could catch up with them. He could only hope they would double back in their tracks. 'Ace!' he muttered anxiously. He jogged on.

Midge's room was thick with dust. A coffee cup left half-empty months before sat thickly by the bed. No one had disturbed anything since his departure. Posters for heavy metal bands hung off the walls. A cracked mirror sat crookedly on a battered chest of drawers.

The Master stared at his own reflection. Behind him Midge crouched on the bed, curled protectively round himself, shaking. His yellow eyes stared at nothing. Torn between two worlds and two identities, he trembled.

In the mirror the Master saw that his own eyes had flooded with yellow. He shut them quickly. 'I will be free of this,' he muttered fiercely. He opened his eyes again. They were still cat's eyes. 'I will be free of this!' he repeated with greater vehemence.

Slowly the yellow ebbed out of his eyes. The Master smiled. He looked again at Midge, quivering, witless, his lead trailing from his neck and the smile faded.

'You are all animal now,' he whispered, though Midge made no sign of hearing him. 'You are so weak; your will is devoured. A strong mind will hold onto itself longer – a will as strong as mine. He looked in the mirror again. 'How long?' he asked his own reflection. For a long moment he stared into his own eyes. His face tightened in anger. 'If I have to suffer this contamination, this . . .' his mouth twisted in disgust, 'humiliation, if I am to become an animal, then like an animal I will destroy you, Doctor. I will hunt you, trap you and destroy you!'

On the planet, it was raining. Hot, heavy drops of water made craters in the dust and turned the rocks to darker shades of red and brown and made them look like fresh blood. Paterson, Shreela and Derek sat in a miserable huddle on the brow of the hill.

Paterson was talking doggedly, a monologue as

regular and monotonous as the downpour. 'On this survival course, SAS it was, we made shelters that could keep out a force ten gale. Dry as bone they were and all we had were four branches, a few leaves and a Swiss army knife.

He paused for some reaction. Derek had not heard a word; he was listening to whatever rhythm kept him rocking to and fro. Shreela was trying to ignore them both. Paterson managed to catch her eye.

'Initiative – a few basic skills and a bit of initiative, that's all you need.'

Shreela stared at him. 'Have you got a Swiss army knife?'

Paterson fidgeted nervously. 'Well, not on me but . . .'

Shreela sighed and looked away.

Ace stood with her face turned up to the sky, letting the warm water run into her mouth. She laughed and looked over at Karra. The Cheetah woman's fur was sodden; she caught rain drops on the tip of her pink tongue. Her eyes were shut.

'I thought cats hated the rain,' said Ace.

Karra opened her eyes. 'I'm not a cat,' she said softly. 'I'm Karra; I'm your sister.'

Ace blinked at her. 'No you're not.' Karra didn't answer, she just watched Ace steadily. 'Why do you call me that?'

'You're like me,' purred Karra.

'Yeah?'

'You will be.'

Ace smiled uncertainly. 'This is good. I like feeling like this.' She looked down and frowned. Crouching, she peered at herself in the puddles at their feet. She knew there was something strange about her reflection which she watched as it steadied out of ripples. There was something about her eyes but she couldn't remember what.

'Where's the Doctor?'

Karra didn't answer. Looking up, Ace saw her sniffing the air. 'Are you hungry?' Karra asked softly.

Ace peered again at her own face. 'I've got to get back to the Doctor,' she muttered.

'The chase.' Karra's voice had a growl in it.

'What?'

'The hunt. Smell the blood on the wind.' Karra raised her head and drew a long breath. 'Hear the blood in your ears, run, run beyond the horizon and catch your hunger.' She gave a long purring yowl.

There was the sound of hoofs. Ace looked round and saw two horses trotting towards them.

Karra laughed. 'Are you hungry, sister?' She ran to the nearest horse and jumped on its back. Looking back at Ace she bared her teeth in a grin. 'Come hunting.'

Ace's face broke into a grin of her own. She ran to the other horse and pulled herself on to its back. In a thunder of hoofs and dust they galloped back across the plain, Ace's whoop trailing behind them.

The Master had turned from the mirror to pace restlessly round the room. Either the Doctor would die on the other side of the galaxy or he would return here. However it turned out, the Master would be the instrument of his destruction. The Master smiled.

The front door of the flat slammed. He turned abruptly towards the sound. He could hear a woman's voice in the hall, a child answering and the rustle of plastic bags. He looked at Midge. The boy was still lost in his own wilderness, unhearing and unseeing.

The Master moved swiftly over and gripped his shoulders.

'Look at me,' he whispered imperatively. 'Look at me!'

Slowly Midge looked up and focused on the Master's eyes, cat's eyes again like his own.

'You have power. We have power now.' The Master's will flooded out of his eyes and into Midge. The boy had no other thoughts left.

'Yeah,' agreed Midge. His shaking stopped.

'You can do anything you want now. Anything.'

Midge began to smile. 'Yes.'

The Master smiled back. 'You're my hunting dog, Midge, the teeth of my trap.' Midge blinked at him, confused.

The Master's smile broadened. 'Trust me Midge,' he said softly. He looked in the direction of the voices in the hall.

A kitling leapt out of the wall and walked towards them.

The animal was dead. It lay on the ground with its throat torn out, its great horns curving above its head into the dust. Karra had already dismounted and was walking towards it.

Ace watched her. She was confused. She remembered the animal's speed and power as they pursued it. She heard again the heavy thunder of its hoofs, its snorting breath and the hot smell of its fear as they galloped close. Now it was dead.

She looked at it. She felt as though its power had flowed into her, as if she and Karra had seized that when they caught the animal. She thought it wasn't dead: it lay there for her to eat and then it would be alive again, all that strength and speed alive in her bones and muscles. 'Good hunting,' she whispered.

Karra looked up and grinned in agreement.

It suddenly occurred to Ace that she had never eaten raw meat. The thought was disturbing. She had a sudden vision of Karra's fierce, toothy face as she had leapt on the buffalo – as she had leapt on Stuart's back.

'You kill people,' she said. 'You eat people.'

Karra turned to look at her again. 'When I'm hungry, I hunt. When I hunt, I eat.' She watched Ace seriously.

'Would you eat me?'

Karra considered for a moment. She pointed at the dead animal. 'There is meat here.'

'But if there wasn't,' Ace persisted, 'would you eat me?'

Karra smiled. 'How fast can you run, sister?'

Ace swallowed. 'Fast enough,' she said quietly.

Karra drew a slow breath of satisfaction. 'Aaah. That would be a good hunt.' She smiled at Ace again. 'Are you hungry? Come and eat.' She turned back to their kill, crouching over it.

Ace slipped off her horse and went to join her.

The Doctor's voice froze her in her tracks.

'Ace.'

She turned and saw him standing against the sky behind them. He held out his hand. 'Ace, come back.'

With cat's eyes, Ace squinted at him. She was caught between two thoughts, her mind a blank. She was not certain she recognized him. She looked at Karra.

The Cheetah woman was also watching the Doctor, half crouched and wary. She didn't move.

'Come home, Ace,' the Doctor called urgently.

103

As Ace watched, Karra seemed to change. She suddenly saw a half human, half animal creature with blood around its jaws. She gasped.

Karra turned to her; Ace stepped back. Karra showed her teeth. It no longer looked like a grin. It was a bloody snarl.

Ace turned on her heel and pelted up the slope towards the Doctor. She grabbed him in a terrified hug.

'What's happening to me, Doctor?'

The Doctor patted her back soothingly, staring steadily back at Karra. 'It's all right. We're going home now.'

Karra turned away from them and began to feed.

It was a Monday morning, but the Perivale minimarket was still deserted. Harvey leaned on one side of the counter, disgruntledly running a filthy duster over the keys of the till. Len leaned on the other side and chewed thoughtfully on something that had caught in his back teeth.

Harvey shook his head. 'I don't know, Len, I can feel it.'

Len stopped chewing. 'What?'

'The wall at my back.'

Len glanced at the wall behind the till, opened his mouth and then appeared to think better of it. 'Went up the doctor's about my back the other day,' he offered.

Harvey went on dusting. 'What did he say?' he asked without much interest.

'Said it was evolution.'

Harvey stopped dusting. 'You what?'

Len leaned more heavily on the counter, wagging his finger for emphasis. 'Said we, as in homo sapiens,

104

had not evolved sufficiently yet to walk on our hind legs in comfort. Might take another couple of millennia he said – gave me some paracetamol in the meantime.'

'What did you say to him?' asked Harvey.

'I wondered if fifteen years bolting cars together might've done a bit of damage. He said it probably hadn't helped.' Len recommenced chewing reflectively. 'That and evolution, my spinal column had no chance.'

Harvey opened the till. 'Look at that. Didn't even bother taking the dosh out last night.' He raked his hand over a meagre collection of coins and notes. 'How're you supposed to keep up with all the punters getting everything they want from the flipping supermarket?'

Len stroked his moustache thoughtfully. 'Yeah, it's a funny thing . . .'

Harvey interrupted. 'Everything they want and a little bit more? Might have left me the little bit more, eh?'

Len nodded. 'A funny thing, evolution.'

The door to the shop banged open, clattering the bell. Both men looked round. They stared at a young man in battered clothes. His skin was streaked with dirt and what looked like dried blood. He had a pair of dark glasses perched on his nose.

Midge stopped, looking back at them.

Len gave a low whistle of disbelief. 'Look at the state of this one.'

Harvey cleared his throat. 'Can I help you son?' It was the tone of a bouncer about to assist a client out onto the pavement.

Midge walked slowly up to the till. 'I need a suit of clothes and a haircut.' He made it sound like a command.

Harvey and Len looked at each other and burst out laughing. 'Took the words right out of my mouth, son,' spluttered Harvey. 'But I don't think you've come to the right place, somehow.'

Midge took off his dark glasses. Harvey's laugh died in his throat. Midge's eyes glared at him – the yellow eyes of a cat.

Harvey coughed nervously. 'Have you seen a doctor about that, son?'

Midge didn't blink. 'Give me the money,' he said softly.

Len straightened himself up ready for trouble; Harvey slammed the till drawer shut and folded his arms aggressively.

'No way.'

The shop bell rang again. They all turned to see the Master standing by the door. He was a dark shadowy figure against the bright shelves.

'What do you want, Midge?' he said.

Midge still glared at Harvey. 'He's got to give me the money,' he repeated.

The Master smiled and his eyes flooded with yellow. Harvey and Len stepped back. Their hands dropped to their sides; their faces went slack. They couldn't have looked away if they'd tried.

The Master took a step forward. 'Give him the money,' he hissed.

Without taking his eyes off The Master's, Harvey opened the till. Its bell rang loudly in the silence. Harvey removed a wad of notes and handed them to Midge.

The Master smiled again. 'Midge must have anything he wants. Midge has special powers, don't you Midge?'

106

Midge was absorbed in counting his money with eager greed.

The Master moved closer to him. As he came into the light it became clear he had a kitling curled in his arms. Its red eyes were half shut as he petted it.

'Is that all you want Midge?'

Midge looked up bemusedly. The Master sighed. 'What repulsively petty little ambitions you have, Midge. I will have to broaden your horizons. Do you know what you are?'

Midge shook his head. Behind him Harvey and Len still stood transfixed.

'You're my hunting dog, Midge,' murmured the Master. 'You're the teeth of my trap and you're going to do exactly as I say, aren't you?'

Midge nodded eagerly, his eyes fixed on his money.

The Master patted him soothingly as if calming an excited dog. 'Because you're powerful, Midge, very, very powerful. We must get you anything you want.' He turned and ushered Midge out of the shop. Harvey and Len stirred as his gaze turned away from them. The Master swung back. The kitling leapt out of his arms and straight at Harvey, its eyes blazing.

Harvey flung up his arms protectively. 'Len! Len! Get it!' he yelled. Len grabbed a broom.

The kitling hit Harvey; Len hit it. All three vanished.

Chuckling softly, the Master closed the door on the deserted shop.

On the planet, Shreela, Paterson and Derek sat in a damp huddle watching the Doctor and Ace who were deep in discussion. None of them had spoken to Ace since the Doctor had brought her back to them, pale and silent. Shreela watched Ace's face anxiously. Her eyes appeared normal now, but was she really unchanged? Was she still Ace?

The Doctor put his hands on Ace's shoulders. 'Ace, look at me.' She did so. 'Now relax and try to make your mind a blank.' He felt her shoulders sag under his hands. The lines of tension vanished from her face and the yellow light of the Cheetah People crept back into her eyes. 'You're possessed, Ace,' he went on softly. 'It's the planet – the Cheetah People. You've changed.'

Ace nodded slowly. 'Yes.'

'You're powerful, dangerous.'

'Yes.'

'If you stay here, the change will accelerate. If you leave you may never be the same again. If you use your powers to leave this place, to fight, to defend yourself – for anything – the change may accelerate.'

'Yes.'

'If you try to leap off this world it will increase its hold on you, but the rest of us are trapped here unless you help us escape.'

Ace blinked. She remembered Midge, snarling on his leather lead, leaping for home and taking the Master with him. She remembered the Master's scornful words. 'He doesn't remember his name.' She focused on the Doctor again. He was watching her gravely, waiting.

'What should I do Professor?'

He shook his head.

'Tell me,' she persisted. 'I trust you.'

He shook his head again. 'It's your choice, Ace.'

Ace watched him for a second with her animal eyes before she broke into a grin. She held out her hand. The Doctor smiled back, took her hand, and held out his other one to Shreela. Shreela's face brightened as she guessed what they were up to. She caught Derek's hand. Finally, reluctantly, Paterson joined himself to Derek and the human chain. Like children about to play ring-a-roses, they stood looking expectantly at Ace. The Doctor squeezed her hand.

'Lets go home, Ace.'

Ace broke into a run. She looked back at the line of people that she was pulling after her and laughed as if it were a game. She jumped into the air.

The wind blew the dust over the empty hill-top; there was nothing human left.

Chapter 7

Midge stood looking at his reflection in the plate-glass window of a motorcycle showroom. He liked what he saw. His hair was freshly and stylishly cut and he had a new set of clothes. He stroked the heavy, expensive material appreciatively. It was black – he was all in black like the figure that watched him from the other side of the street: the Master, the man who put the thoughts in his head and gave him what he wanted.

He liked what he saw inside the showroom as well: A row of gleaming, powerful bikes, leaning quietly on their stands. He wanted one.

There were two men in the back office of the showroom. One talked on the phone; the other was busy with paperwork. Midge eyed them carefully. He turned back to the Master who still watched steadily from across the street. His instruction was clear. It was so simple. Midge grinned and pushed open the door of the showroom.

The TARDIS was still standing on an empty street, empty until Ace, the Doctor and the others appeared out of thin air beside it. For a few seconds, none of them moved. They blinked at the bright, familiar world that had been so suddenly restored to them. Ace turned to the Doctor. Her gaze was slightly questioning as if she no longer remembered how they had got here. And her eyes were their usual colour again.

Shreela laughed with delight, waving her arm at the whole street. 'We're back! We're home!'

Derek and Paterson still stood hand in hand. They were stunned. Each wore an identical blank expression.

Shreela turned to Ace and gave her a brief, hard hug. 'I've got to get back home!' She pelted off down the street.

Paterson suddenly noticed he was still clutching Derek's hand. He dropped it abruptly. 'What's your game then?' he demanded, eyes popping in outrage.

He backed off and stared at them suspiciously. A frantic look on his face suggested he was casting around desperately for rational explanations. He appeared to find one.

'So I had a blackout,' he spluttered. 'Perfectly normal – stress, overwork, that's all. I've had medicals, sound as a bell I am.' He slapped his chest. 'Sound as a bell. Did you get a doctor? Should've got a doctor to me though, that's the least you could've done, instead of keeping me lying about in the street.'

He pointed an accusing finger at the Doctor. 'You are a doctor, right? You should know better.'

Ace folded her arms and stared at him. 'Thanks, Ace,' she spat out, her voice heavy with sarcasm, 'thanks Doctor, thanks for saving my life, getting me safe home.'

'Don't know what you're talking about,' Paterson retorted nervously. He looked down at his torn and

111

mud-stained uniform and brushed at it ineffectually. Whatever it suggested to him he was not prepared to consider it. 'I'm late for self-defence,' he muttered. He turned and walked off with a brisk and determined march.

Derek looked at Paterson, Ace and the Doctor. A sane and human smile spread across his face. 'Thanks,' he said quietly. He ran off in another direction.

Ace shook herself as if she was waking up. 'Looks like everything's back to normal,' she beamed at the Doctor. She turned towards the TARDIS. It looked like home. She patted it affectionately.

The Doctor was still looking up and down the road, a puzzled frown on his face. Ace sighed impatiently.

'Come on, Professor. What do we want to hang around here for?'

'Unfinished business,' murmured the Doctor.

'What unfinished business?'

The Doctor looked at her seriously. 'The Master.'

Ace snorted. 'What would he still be hanging round the dump of the universe for?'

'You were the one . . .' began the Doctor.

'. . . who wanted to come home,' finished Ace. 'Yeah, yeah. Heard it. Listen,' she banged the side of the TARDIS again, 'this is the only home I've got now, OK?'

The Doctor stared at her intently for a moment. 'Yes, you brought us here, home.' He looked at the TARDIS. 'So Midge would – where does he live?'

Ace gaped. 'Who?'

'Midge!' The Doctor was getting impatient.

'I don't know. He used to be in those flats there.' Ace pointed at a couple of high-rise blocks that loomed over the semi-detached houses.

The Doctor instantly set off at a brisk walk. He glanced back over his shoulder. 'Well, come on!'

Ace stared at the cat that had come to sun itself at the door of the TARDIS. It was a red-eyed kitling. They looked at each other for a long moment.

'Ace!' The Doctor's voice was receding.

Ace shook herself and ran after the Doctor.

In the bike showroom, Midge was sitting on a monster machine, still dazed with the thrill of possession. Behind him, the office was empty; the two salesmen had vanished. The telephone receiver hung off the cradle where one of them had let it fall. As Midge caressed the handlebars of the machine, he whispered the words that were being fed into his brain. 'This is just the start, Midge, just the start.' He laughed. His yellow eyes turned to stare out the window.

On the other side of the street the Master still stood staring back. Midge nodded slowly. 'Yeah,' he whispered. 'Yeah, I know what to do.'

Midge's room had not become any cleaner since his recent return. Ace wrinkled her nose at the dust and the coffee cups. She surveyed Midge's collection of heavy metal posters and raised a contemptuous eyebrow. 'Is he still into that lot? I'd have thought they'd be drawing their pensions by now.'

The Doctor was looking at something on the floor – a battered, furry remnant. He was about to move closer when a sound from the hall stopped him.

A little girl stood in the doorway, watching them. Her face was streaked with dust and tears. She looked about eight. She stared at them mournfully, sniffing to herself.

Ace dropped to crouch beside her. 'What's up?' she asked.

The girl sniffed again. 'My cat,' she whispered.

Ace looked towards the Doctor and saw him studying the furry remnant on the floor. He looked up at her and nodded. It was the cat.

Ace put a gentle arm round the girl's shoulder. 'What happened?'

'The bad cat ate it. The bad cat the man brought.' The girl stared at her with big, blank, shocked eyes.

'What man!' The Doctor's voice was sharp. The girl drew away from him. He crouched like Ace, softening his tone. 'Can you tell us where he went? It's very important.'

In the community centre, the training room was full. The young men were chatting and loosening up before their work-out, pulling off upper layers of track-suits. The sergeant was late. Occasionally, one of the boys looked out the door to see if he was on his way.

So when Midge entered he had the attention of everyone in the room.

He walked into the silence, pulled down the cuffs of his new, expensive suit, and turned his mirrored sunglasses to look at each of them.

'Waiting on the sarge?' he asked pleasantly. No one answered. 'He's been held up. He asked me to have a little chat with you.'

The young men parted to let him walk through.

'I learned a little secret today – the secret of success.' He had reached the front of the room. He turned and grinned at his silent audience. 'I thought I'd share it with you.'

* * *

The Doctor and Ace stood on the balcony outside Midge's flat. Ace had the little girl by the hand. Below them stray cats squabbled over uncollected rubbish sacks. The girl pointed up the road. 'Up there,' she said. 'Midge and the bad cat man.'

Ace and the Doctor exchanged an anxious look.

'Midge went away, then he came back,' continued the little girl. 'He's my big brother. He's got funny eyes now.'

Ace bent over her. 'Where's your mum, Squeak?'

The girl's face trembled but her voice remained emotionless. 'She saw the bad cat man. He made her go away.'

Ace straightened up, shaking with fury. 'What's he doing it for?' she exploded. 'Why?! He's escaped hasn't he? He doesn't need to keep the Cheetah People busy – he's safe! What's he still doing it for!?'

The Doctor's mouth tightened. 'Malice,' he said bitterly.

Ace bent and picked up the little girl. 'Her gran's on the next floor up, I'll take her there.' She paused, holding the child. 'Why is he still hanging around here?'

'He hates me,' the Doctor said warily. 'He must hope – believe – he's found something . . .' the Doctor sighed then continued, 'something to destroy me.'

Ace snorted. 'You'd wipe the floor with him.'

The Doctor looked down at the scavenging cats and frowned. 'Not necessarily. We are very much alike, the Master and I. We're different sides of the same coin – balanced, equal. We've always been an explosive combination. One of us may one day very well blot the other out.' He ran his hand over his face. 'If we could only track him down, surprise him before he's ready.'

115

Ace gasped. Turning sharply to look at her, the Doctor was just in time to see her eyes flood with yellow. She gazed fixedly ahead. The girl raised her hand and touched Ace's cheek. 'Bad cat man,' she whispered.

Outside the community centre, the Master stood motionless. His cat's eyes stared at what his inner eye showed him. 'Ace,' he whispered. 'Ace.'

Ace had put the little girl down. Her yellow eyes stared past the balcony. 'He's at the community centre,' she said softly.

As the Doctor watched, the yellow colour left her eyes. She blinked at him, bemused. 'He's at the community centre, I know he is.'

The Doctor nodded. 'Take the girl upstairs first,' he said, 'then we'll go after him.'

Midge's mirrored lenses turned this way and that over his audience. They were all watching him, listening, but they were becoming restless. They scowled and glanced at each other.

'It's common sense, right?' he urged them. 'It's just the way of the world, right? Survival of the fittest, get rid of the dead wood, let the wasters go to the wall and the strong will inherit the earth. You and me will inherit the earth.'

The other boys considered this; they did not appear particularly impressed.

'Do you hear what I'm saying?' demanded Midge. 'Do you know what I'm talking about?'

No one responded. With one swift movement Midge pulled off his glasses. Yellow eyes glared at the other young men. They gasped and stepped back, looking at each other in shock.

'Don't move!' commanded Midge.

One of the heaviest and most muscular of the men stepped forward and squared his jaw aggressively.

'Don't move.' This time the command was gentle, barely audible. It came from the other side of the room. Turning, the young men confronted the Master, who stood motionless behind them, his yellow eyes glaring. As his gaze picked out one face after another the men relaxed; their jaws went slack; their eyes glazed over.

'Come here,' the Master said softly, still gazing at them compellingly.

'Come here!' ordered Midge. His voice was loud and aggressive.

Mesmerized, the young men turned to look at him. They listened to the words the Master dictated that issued as commands from Midge's mouth.

'You understand me,' whispered the Master.

'You understand me!' Midge repeated loudly, looking commandingly at them all.

'You'll do anything I say.' The Master moved among them, looking at them all appraisingly.

'You'll do anything I say,' repeated Midge. All the young men were watching him.

'Won't you?' the Master said gently.

'Won't you!' demanded Midge.

All the young men snapped to attention. 'Yes, sarge!' they chorused. Midge smiled.

The door into the training room opened. Paterson limped in. He had tried to clean himself up a bit but he was still wearing his battered uniform. All the young men turned to look at him. They stood in a solid pack, blocking his view of Midge and the Master.

Paterson shuffled towards them, head down. He spoke hesitantly.

'OK lads, sorry I was held up but, eh, well duty calls you know. Right . . .' He looked up for the first time. His team of boys stared coldly back at him. Paterson made a strained attempt at enthusiasm. 'Well, come on then!' He clapped his hands. 'Let's get moving, let's get a bit of sweat going here, you know what I always say . . .' His voice died away.

The young men parted as if on command to reveal Midge and the Master. Paterson blinked nervously and stared into Midge's yellow eyes.

'There's no room for shirkers, no room for dead wood,' said Midge pleasantly. 'Isn't that what you always say, sarge?'

Paterson looked at the blank, hostile faces of his training team and began to back off.

The Master smiled. 'Why don't you take over now, Midge?' he suggested.

As they ran towards the community centre, Ace was aware of a tugging sense of urgency in her stomach. She knew something terrible was happening. She increased her speed and pounded along the pavement; the Doctor matched her pace. They crashed through the doors of the centre, rattling the cracked glass.

Without breaking stride they hit the door of the training room. They burst into the room and abruptly skidded to a halt on the polished floor.

Paterson was sprawled in the centre of the room, staring sightlessly at the ceiling. He appeared to have been battered to death.

The Doctor shook his head sadly. 'So much for the SAS survival course,' he murmured.

Ace gasped and clutched his arm. Her eyes had

118

flooded with yellow again. The Doctor gripped her shoulders. 'Where?' he demanded.

Ace looked at him in horror. 'Derek,' she whispered.

Derek was playing happily outside his home. He kicked a ball off the wall and dribbled it round the parked cars. The ball escaped him and rolled away. It collided with the front wheel of a stationary motor-bike. Derek looked up.

Midge sat on the back of his giant machine, his cat's eyes crinkling as he gave a toothy smile. 'You got a minute, Derek?' he said softly.

Derek gaped in terror and turned to run. He stopped. Behind him the self-defence team was spread out across the road. The men were still in their training gear but their soft shoes had been exchanged for heavy boots. They smiled at him but there was no comfort in their expressions.

Behind them, like a shepherd guiding his flock, stood the Master. He raised his arms. The pack of men moved towards Derek. Midge revved his engine.

The street appeared to be empty as Ace and the Doctor ran down it. Ace yelled at the top of her lungs, 'Derek! Derek!' She stopped short; the Doctor nearly cannoned into her.

Derek's body was lying in a crumpled heap in the middle of the road. There was no doubt that he was dead.

'He's leaving a trail,' muttered the Doctor, 'like a paper chase – a trail of bodies.'

Ace stared past Derek; her eyes had turned again. 'That way,' she said quietly and led the way past the crumpled body towards the waste-ground at the other end of the road.

The waste-ground was deserted. Pink heads of willow herb nodded peacefully in the warm wind. On its own in the centre of the empty ground stood a huge, black motorbike. Ace walked up to it and put her hand on the warm leather of the seat.

'The trail stops here.' She stood, uncertain, her yellow eyes looking at nothing.

The Doctor sighed heavily. 'He's chosen the time and the place.' He sat down on the bike and looked at the empty landscape. 'Might as well get comfortable before the curtain goes up.'

Ace turned her head as if her cat's eyes were now blind. 'The trail stops here,' she repeated.

'Ace,' the Doctor said gently.

She looked at him; gradually the yellow faded out of her eyes.

'That's better,' said the Doctor.

She blinked at him. 'Did I go again?' she asked miserably. The Doctor nodded. 'I don't even feel it. I don't even feel myself change, Professor. Am I going to stay like this?'

Before the Doctor could answer they were interrupted by the roar of an approaching motorbike behind them.

Chapter 8

Midge bumped slowly towards them over a rise in the rough ground. The defence group jogged behind him in tight formation, all their feet hitting the ground at the same time; each face was set in the same menacing glower.

Midge brought the bike to a halt about two hundred yards from the Doctor and Ace. His intention was obvious: the two black bikes were lined up facing each other like horses at a medieval joust.

The group stared silently at the Doctor and Ace. The Master moved through the ranks of the defence group to stand by Midge. He stared with cat's eyes at his prey. Ace's eyes were yellow as she glared back.

'You're my hunting dog, Midge,' murmured the Master, 'the teeth of my trap, the teeth to destroy!' The Master took out the carnivore's tooth that Midge had killed with on the planet and put it into his hand. Midge bared his own teeth as he clutched it and crouched low over the handlebars. His smart suit clung tightly to his body; his cat's eyes blazed as he revved the engine.

As if it were a cue, Ace leapt on to the other bike to face him, snarling in her turn.

'Stay out of this, Ace!'

The Doctor pulled her from the saddle. She was still staring across at Midge. The Doctor grabbed and shook her.

'Ace, listen to me! Listen to me!' Slowly she turned to look at him. 'You mustn't fight. Do you understand? You must not fight! You'd change. Can you hear me, Ace? You'd change for ever!'

Ace stared at him with her alien, expressionless eyes. Slowly, she nodded. The yellow faded from her eyes. She shivered. 'OK, Professor.' Her voice was low and serious.

She watched as the Doctor got on the bike to face Midge across the field. 'But that's what the Master wants – he wants you,' she said.

The Doctor looked at her for a second and shrugged resignedly. He reached up, took off his hat and handed it to her. He winked, and kicked the bike into life.

Engines throbbing, the two machines faced each other. The Doctor looked past Midge to the Master and saw his enemy's mouth curl in a cruel, satisfied smile. The Master raised his hand and let it drop. Midge's motorbike leapt forward; the Doctor accelerated to meet him.

The two bikes rushed at each other, head on, both riders crouched low on the machines. Ace saw Midge's face was disfigured by a grinning snarl. He rushed closer and closer to the Doctor. She waited for one machine to dodge or swerve. It wasn't going to happen.

'NO!' screamed Ace.

The end of her scream was lost in the explosion. A

flash of orange flame leapt to the sky. Ace turned her face away, blinded. There was another explosion. She looked back.

The wreckage of the two bikes lay in a tangled heap of mutilated metal in the centre of the field. The ground around them was scorched and smouldering. The bikes were still blazing. Midge's charred body moved feebly to one side of the wreck. There was no sign of the Doctor.

Ace took a step forward, clutching the Doctor's hat to her chest. 'No,' she whispered hopelessly.

On the ground, Midge struggled to crawl forward. The Master watched him impassively; the defence group observed Midge with their mindless, brutal stare.

'Survival of the fittest,' murmured the Master. 'The weak must be eliminated so that the healthy can flourish.

Every head in the defence group slowly turned to look at him. The Master stared back with his command blazing from his eyes.

'Well?' he said.

The defence group broke into a trot and converged on the crippled Midge, their boots pounding on the ground.

Ace stepped back in horror as she guessed their purpose.

Midge raised his face from the ground, saw the approaching boots and gaped in terror. They surrounded him.

'Stop it!' screamed Ace. 'Stop it!'

It was already over. The defence group broke out of their kicking cluster and formed a solid line again, moving slowly towards Ace. Behind them, Midge's battered body was motionless.

The group stepped in unison – a slow march which brought them closer and closer to Ace. She could see their blank faces. Only the Master's will commanded them. And their purpose was to destroy her.

Ace began to back off, muttering to herself, 'I must not fight. I must not fight!' She looked down at the Doctor's hat in her hands and searched around desperately.

'Doctor?' she called. There was no help for her – only the boots bearing down on her.

'DOCTOR!?' she yelled.

She saw the Master smile. She looked round again wildly. There was nowhere to run to, and for the first time in her life she could not stand and fight.

'Help me!' she shouted. She screamed again in desperation to anyone or anything that could hear, 'Somebody HELP ME!'

There was a rushing in the air behind her. She saw the defence group stop. They looked above her head and were suddenly terrified. Ace turned to look behind her.

A horse towered over her and on the horse was Karra. Ace's call had been heard.

Karra raised herself on the horse's back and sat posed and motionless. Her teeth gleamed.

'The Chase,' she said softly. 'To hunt in the morning and live until evening, run out of the light and slip into the dark, smell the blood on the wind, hear your blood in your ears, die at last with your enemies' blood in your mouth.'

No one moved. Ace watched spellbound; the defence group was frozen in terror; the Master's face was tight with fury.

Karra's muscles rippled beneath her fur as she leaned slowly forward. 'With your enemies' blood in your mouth,' she repeated. She threw back her head and gave a purring howl. She charged.

The defence group scattered. Karra spurred her horse at each of them in turn, driving them screaming and stumbling across the waste-ground. Her teeth gleamed in her lean face; her claws raked at their heads and backs. The horse pranced in a rearing circle, kicking up dust with its heavy hoofs. As it settled there was no one left in the field apart from Karra, Ace and the Master. The last of the young men was scampering out of sight in the distance.

Karra turned to the Master. He had remained silent and motionless, a sinister dark figure waiting for her approach. She charged at him past Midge's body, thundering down on him with her teeth bared. He did not move. Karra brought the horse to a skidding halt within feet of him. He looked up at her impassively. His eyes were as yellow as hers but they seemed to bore into her, commanding her.

'Get off your horse,' he commanded quietly. Karra hesitated. 'Get off your horse!' he shouted at her, suddenly steely.

Ace gasped as she saw the Cheetah women obey. Karra stood in front of the Master, apparently submissive.

'You have no power here,' said the Master. 'This is not your place. I command her; I command you. You have no power over me.'

Karra listened, motionless, her head on one side. She seemed mesmerized.

'I can do anything I wish with you and you can do nothing – nothing – to me.'

Karra stirred at last. 'Do you bleed?' she purred.

For the first time the Master's pose was shaken. He

125

stared at her, unable to believe she was not in his power.

'I can always do something to you,' continued Karra conversationally, 'if you bleed.'

The Master took a hesitant step back, still gaping at her. Karra howled again. She sprang and the Master ran.

He ducked round her and ran towards Ace. He sped past Midge's corpse, briefly bending and snatching something from the dead boy's hand. Karra was nearly on his back. Her muscles uncoiled for a final spring.

Ace saw Midge's tooth knife in the Master's hand.

'Karra!' she screamed.

Karra sprang.

The Master turned and drove the knife into her chest. Karra fell forward as the Master turned and continued his flight. Karra dropped to her knees and then onto her face. She briefly clawed at the knife and lay still.

Hidden now by a rise in the ground, the Master heard Ace's desolate wail.

'Karra!'

The Master grinned in satisfaction. Brushing down his clothes he turned to walk away.

There was an arm sticking out from a heap of rubbish sacks nearby, an arm that wore a familiar sleeve. Moving closer, the Master saw the Doctor's body lying motionless under heaps of split rubbish sacks. He stirred the body with his foot. There was no response, no movement and no breath. Some rotting potato peelings tumbled on to the Doctor's face. The Master began to smile again, a smile that broadened to a grin. He began to laugh, first a chuckle

126

and then a deep belly laugh that continued as he walked away. The sound followed him out of sight.

In a shower of tea-bags, bean cans and potato peel, the Doctor erupted out of the rubbish sacks and glared after the Master. 'O very good,' he growled. 'Very amusing.' He got up and followed the other Time Lord.

Karra lay on her face in the dirt. Ace could see the blood spreading out from underneath her. She ran to her and pulled her on to her back. She gasped.

Karra's eyes looked back at her, they were still yellow but there was no fur on her face – no canines in her mouth. Her face was the face of a young woman the same age as Ace; the hands that gripped Ace's arms had fingers, not claws. Ace saw that the woman she held was completely human, and that she was dying.

Karra's lips moved. Ace bent her head to catch the words. 'I can hunt in the dark.'

It was still Karra's voice, still the face of the strange wild woman who had called her sister. Ace felt pain in her own chest – the heavy weight of loss.

'I'll get you water,' she said urgently. 'I'll make you well again.' But she knew there was no moon water here.

'I can run into the dark, run for ever,' repeated Karra. She groaned suddenly, her face crumpled in pain.

'Just wait!' pleaded Ace. 'I'll get you something!'

Karra shook her head slowly. She smiled. 'Good hunting, sister.' Her voice was barely audible.

Ace barely felt the tears that flooded down her face. 'Good hunting, sister,' she whispered in reply.

The yellow ebbed out of Karra's eyes and revealed

them to be a clear and sightless blue. Karra was dead. Slowly, Ace reached out and stroked Karra's face as she had once touched her fur by a lake on another planet.

The Master was pressed against the door of the TARDIS. He was busy picking its lock, a task that required all his concentration and a variety of instruments that resembled no earthly lock-pick. Behind him, someone cleared his throat. The Master turned.

The Doctor stood with his thumbs behind his braces, one eyebrow raised quizzically. 'Good hunting, Master?'

The Master snarled in disbelief.

Ace walked quickly away from the waste-ground, tears still rolling unnoticed down her face.

'Ace?'

Ace turned. Shreela was standing on the other side of the road looking at her uncertainly. She quickly rubbed a hand across her face as she waited for the other girl to cross over to her.

'Where's the Doctor?' asked Shreela.

'I don't know,' Ace said bleakly. She looked down at the battered white hat she still clutched. 'Oh, he'll be OK. He'll turn up – he always does.'

Her own words did not seem to reassure her. She continued to stare at the hat which she proceeded to knead. Her face was white and drawn.

'Are you OK?' Shreela put a gentle hand on her arm.

Ace looked up at her. She gave a faint smile. 'Are you?'

Shreela looked away. When she spoke again her voice was quiet. 'Was it real, all that?'

'Oh yeah.' Ace looked at her sympathetically.

Shreela shuddered. 'They think I lost my memory, my family. I feel as if I have – I'm pretending I dreamed it.'

Ace nodded. 'Yeah, best way.' As she spoke she realized she no longer had that choice. She had seen too much that was strange, terrifying and wonderful since she left home – since she met the Doctor. She could not forget; she would never be at home in Perivale again.

'Are you going away again?' asked Shreela.

Ace nodded. 'Wherever he goes, wherever he is.' She looked down again at the hat she held.

'Are you ever coming back again?'

'No, I don't think so.'

Shreela frowned. She was concerned. 'But what if you can't find him?' she asked.

Ace glared at her. 'If he was dead there'd be a body, right?' she said fiercely.

Shreela looked at her blankly, not understanding what she was talking about.

Ace answered her own question. 'Right!'

She turned and started to stride purposefully back to the waste-ground. She checked herself and turned back to Shreela. 'Your dad's got a car, yeah?' Shreela nodded. 'Could you get me a can of petrol?'

Shreela frowned again. 'What for?'

Ace looked back at the waste-ground. 'One last bonfire,' she said quietly. 'For old times' sake.'

The Master had recovered his composure. He moved towards the Doctor and smiled faintly.

'Yes, it would have been too easy,' he said. 'I was almost disappointed. I have anticipated your death for so long my dear Doctor, I'm delighted it can still be a spectacular farewell.'

'I hate goodbyes,' the Doctor said lightly, but his eyes never left the Master's.

'It seems we always meet again,' mused the Master. 'Eternally bound together, we meet across the universe and fight and meet again, over and over.'

'They do say that opposites attract,' quipped the Doctor. The Master had started to circle him so he took a wary step backwards.

'But this is the end, Doctor.' The Master gave a broad, inhuman grin. Canines snarled in his mouth and his eyes had flooded with yellow. 'Can you see it?' he whispered.

The Doctor nodded.

'It's a power. A power from that planet,' continued the Master. 'It's growing in me. It's ancient, wild and primeval – the oldest force in the universe.'

There was no doubt that the Master was circling the Doctor. He half crouched, his yellow eyes staring hungrily up at the Doctor. The Master licked his pointed teeth.

'Do you understand?' he said. 'An older force than ours – older than the Time Lords. Are you frightened yet, Doctor?'

'No,' said the Doctor calmly, never turning his gaze from the mad yellow eyes.

The Master's grin broadened. 'But you should be. You should be. It nearly beat me, such a simple brutal power, just the power of tooth and claw. It nearly destroyed me, a Time Lord. But I won. I controlled that force, Doctor, and now at last I have the power to destroy you!'

The Master leapt and closed his hands around the Doctor's throat.

★ ★ ★

At first the Doctor was aware only of the choking weight of those hands clenched around his windpipe. As he struggled to break their grip he noticed that the air was hot and full of smoke, that there was beaten earth beneath his feet. He was back on the planet.

He was wrestling his enemy in the centre of the valley, surrounded by spoil-heaps of bones, where the Cheetah People fought their ritual battles.

Part of his mind was aware of all this, and that they were in grave danger. Fissures were opening in the rocks; lava was gushing down gullies: the planet was in its death throes. Most of his mind was consumed by a savage desire to fight, to kill. The power of the planet had never been so strong as it was now when its very substance was breaking up into violence. The Doctor wrestled his enemy with only one thought clearly in his head: to kill before he was killed.

The Master toppled the other Time Lord on to his back. He raised a huge bone, wielding it like a club, ready to bring it crashing down on the Doctor's head. The Doctor threw himself sideways just in time. As the weapon crashed down, its weight pulled the Master off balance. The Doctor pushed him, sending him sprawling, and then pinned the Master's struggling body to the earth. With his free hand he raised the bone club in his turn. He looked into the Master's eyes in the split second before he killed him.

The Doctor paused. He looked round. All the mountains were erupting in great explosions of flame. The air was full of cinders. It was too hot to breath. They were surrounded by Cheetah People, some on horseback, some on foot, all standing gravely watching the fight. As the Doctor paused they turned away as if released. The horses were kicked into a gallop. The other Cheetah People broke into a loping run. All of them leapt . . . and vanished.

The Doctor felt his sanity returning. The planet was dying, all the wild things that could were escaping to new homes, so must they. He lowered his weapon, looking down at the Master. 'Time to go.'

The Master stared back up at him, his eyes still blazing with madness.

'Go where?' he snarled. 'There is no escape except for the animals.' he bared his teeth. 'And I do not choose to live as an animal.' His hands closed again with renewed fury on the Doctor's throat.

As the Doctor fought back he felt rage consume him. He felt his own teeth bared, yellow light flooded his eyes. He tore the Master's hands away.

'If we fight we'll die!' he howled, hardly understanding what he said. 'If we fight we'll die!' He saw the land around them dissolve into flame. With the last bit of himself that remained to him he remembered that he too had somewhere to escape to. He leapt.

Something warm and hard lay under his hands; his whole body was pressed against it. He opened his eyes. He was lying in the road with both arms wrapped round the solid, comforting bulk of the TARDIS. The Doctor laughed with relief. 'Home!' He got up, patting the blue police box affectionately. 'Home.'

He took a deep breath and rubbed his hands over his face. He was alone in the street. Had the Master found his escape or was he too far gone, too consumed already by the savage destruction of the planet? The Doctor sighed again with weary regret.

A window was flung up in a neighbouring house.

Mrs Bates from number thirty-three peered down at him suspiciously.

'Did you hear that racket?' she demanded indignantly. The Doctor blinked inquiringly. 'Did you hear it? Cats. Flipping cat fights all hours of the day.'

The Doctor smiled gently. 'I think you'll find things quietening down now.'

Mrs Bates snorted. 'So you say. Flipping cats – it's the owners I blame: they want the pet, right, they want the animal, but do they keep it under control?'

The Doctor considered. 'We try,' he said.

Mrs Bates snorted again and banged down the window. The Doctor politely raised his hat and went off to find Ace.

Karra lay on the wrecked bikes, her hands crossed across her chest. Midge's knife had been removed and placed between her hands; Midge's body lay at her feet. Karra looked young, wild and beautiful as she lay there. The wind from the fire blew her hair over her closed eyes just before the flames leapt up and hid her from view.

Ace stood watching the pyre, a petrol can dangling from one hand. She was remembering, remembering the feeling of the planet, the power, the wildness. It was dangerous and brutal but it had no malice, a power that had made her as free as Karra. And Karra must once have been a young woman like her.

She heard footsteps behind her. The weight of a familiar hand rested on her shoulder. She smiled, her whole body relaxing in relief, but she did not turn her eyes from the flames. She reached behind her and gave the Doctor back his hat.

'Felt like I could run for ever,' she said softly. 'Felt

like I could smell the wind and feel the grass under my feet and just run for ever.'

'You can never completely leave the planet because you carry it with you inside yourself,' said the Doctor.

Ace smiled. 'Good,' she said. Her face was wet again as she watched the pyre. Smoke and tears blinded her.

'Let's go back to the TARDIS,' the Doctor said gently.

Ace looked up at him.

He smiled at her. 'Let's go home, Ace.'

Arm in arm they walked away.

Postscript

By Peter Darvill-Evans,
Editor of W H Allen's Doctor Who books

Survival, the television story on which this novel is based, was broadcast on BBC1 in Britain between 22 November and 6 December 1989. It was the last Doctor Who story to date; as I write this, in June 1990, the BBC have not yet announced the production plans for further seasons of Doctor Who.

There will be more Target novelizations: three are in preparation now (and there may be others) – all of them based on stories that pre-date *Survival*.

Nonetheless the publication of this book marks an unprecedented event: for the first time since Target novelizations began, we have published the novel of the last televised Doctor Who story, with no immediate prospect of more new stories to novelize.

TARDIS-followers should not despair. We shall continue to publish Target novelizations as long as there are television stories still to be novelized . . .

. . . and, starting some time in the second half of

1991, we shall start to publish new, completely original Doctor Who novels.

The Doctor's adventures will continue onwards – from here; from the end of *Survival*.

SUBSCRIBE TO
DOCTOR WHO MAGAZINE

Every issue of *Doctor Who Magazine* is packed with information about the world's longest running television programme, including news on all the latest Target releases, special reports covering every aspect of the show, merchandise features and a brand new comic strip featuring the current Doctor.

The Magazine is available from newsagents and specialist bookstores — but you can subscribe to thirteen issues of *DWM* for the price of twelve! Just fill out or copy the coupon below, enclose payment for the appropriate amount (made payable to *Marvel Comics Ltd.*) and post it to *Doctor Who Magazine* Subscriptions, PO Box 500, Leicester, Great Britain LE99 0AA. Subscription rates as follows: United Kingdom £18.00; Overseas £30.00; United States, $60.00. Offer expires December 31st 1990 and does not include specials. Please allow 28 days for your subscription to take effect.

Please supply me with *Doctor Who Magazine* for a year commencing with the most recent copy. I will allow 28 days for my subscription to take effect and understand that the subscription does not include any specials.

Please tick your chosen payment method:

☐ I enclose a cheque/postal order for £18.00/£28.00/$60.00 for a year's subscription to *Doctor Who Magazine* made payable to *Marvel Comics Ltd.* This entitles me to thirteen issues for the price of twelve with this voucher.

☐ Please charge £18.00/£28.00/$60.00 to my Visa/Mastercard. My card number is (13 or 16 digits):

Signature ....

Expiry Date ....

Return form and payment to *Doctor Who Magazine* Subscriptions, PO Box 500, Leicester, Great Britain LE99 0AB.

Name ....

Address ....

....

.... Age ....

TARGET (RCP)